EVER SO SOFTLY

Cassandra did not know how long they sat like that, just gazing into each other's eyes, holding each other's hands. But too soon the women's voices grew louder again. Julian was forced to pay attention once more to the sail, in order to steer them safely back to the dock where the boatman was waiting for them.

In silence, they walked back to where her horse stood waiting for her. She turned to say something to him, but he put his finger to her lips. And then he put his own lips to hers in the lightest of kisses that shot chills down her spine and weakened her knees.

He lifted her into the saddle and then ever so softly whispered, "Good night, Cassandra."

Her groom was waiting for her a discreet distance away. She said nothing but gave Julian her secret loving smile, which he returned.

BOOK YOUR PLACE ON OUR WEBSITE AND MAKE THE READING CONNECTION!

We've created a customized website just for our very special readers, where you can get the inside scoop on everything that's going on with Zebra, Pinnacle and Kensington books.

When you come online, you'll have the exciting opportunity to:

- View covers of upcoming books

- Read sample chapters

- Learn about our future publishing schedule (listed by publication month *and author*)

- Find out when your favorite authors will be visiting a city near you

- Search for and order backlist books from our online catalog

- Check out author bios and background information

- Send e-mail to your favorite authors

- Meet the Kensington staff online

- Join us in weekly chats with authors, readers and other guests

- Get writing guidelines

- AND MUCH MORE!

**Visit our website at
http://www.kensingtonbooks.com**

Love of My Life

Meredith Bond

ZEBRA BOOKS
Kensington Publishing Corp.
http://www.kensingtonbooks.com

ZEBRA BOOKS are published by

Kensington Publishing Corp.
850 Third Avenue
New York, NY 10022

All Kensington titles, imprints, and distributed lines are available at special quantity discounts for bulk purchases for sales
promotion, premiums, fund-raising, educational, or institu-
tional use.

Special book excerpts or customized printings can also be created to fit specific needs. For details, write or phone the office
of the Kensington Special Sales Manager: Attn. Special Sales
Department. Kensington Publishing Corp., 850 Third Avenue,
New York, NY 10022. Phone: 1-800-221-2647.

Zebra and the Z logo Reg. U.S. Pat. & TM Off.

ISBN 0-8217-7821-8

First Printing: June 2005
10 9 8 7 6 5 4 3 2 1

Printed in the United States of America

I'd like to thank my editor, Kate Duffy, for being a staunch supporter of Regency books, and for giving me the opportunity to finish my quartet.

And I would like to dedicate this book to my parents-in-law—for their loving support, expertise on all things Indian, and patience (in both relieving me of my ignorance and kindly understanding my disappearances downstairs to write when I should have been visiting with them).

Prologue

London, June 1810

"Oh, where *is* he?" Cassandra strained to see over the heads of the dancers. "He said he would be back momentarily, didn't he, Olivia?"

"Be patient, Cassandra. He has not been gone five minutes!" Olivia Bradmore laughed at her friend and cousin.

Cassandra sat back in her chair and smiled. Her smile grew, until she too was laughing at herself. "You are right, dearest Olivia. I am being a goose! Of course he will be back very soon."

She smoothed the creases from her pale blue gown and adjusted the wide blue velvet ribbon that rested just below her bosom. She was quite thrilled with her gown, knowing that it showed off her eyes and complexion to advantage. She then felt her hair to make sure it was all still properly in place. Thankfully, no loose curls had come out of the intricate arrangement her maid had managed to create.

"My hair hasn't come out of its pins, has it?"

"No, Cassandra, for the fifth time tonight you look absolutely stunning!" Olivia tried not laugh at her friend again, but did shake her head ruefully.

Cassandra took a deep breath and tried to calm herself. "He is being wonderfully attentive this evening, isn't he?"

"Indeed. Much more so than Mr. Saunders has been to me, I'm afraid."

"Oh dear! Poor Olivia! I am so sorry. I have been remarkably selfish. All I have been thinking about has been myself and Lord Felbridge, when you are trying fix your interests with Mr. Saunders."

"Oh no, no, I assure you, I am not so set on Mr. Saunders as you are on Lord Felbridge." Olivia reached out and gave her hand a squeeze. "And your situation is so much more exciting than mine. Why, he might even propose tonight!"

Cassandra sucked in her breath quickly and nearly choked on it. "Do you truly think so? Do you think that is why he asked us to join him here tonight?"

"Well, Vauxhall Gardens is certainly well-known for its romantic walkways. I believe it is quite easy to slip away and have a little privacy," Olivia said. The two girls broke into giggles.

Cassandra stopped quickly, however. "No. No, Olivia, I am certain you are wrong. Why, we have only been in London for a month! It is certainly much too early to be expecting a declaration."

"But you have known each other since last Christmas. Surely you cannot have forgotten all the fun we had with those silly pantomimes?"

"No, how could I ever forget it? It was the most wonderful holiday I've ever had." Cassandra sighed as she remembered how Lord Felbridge had caught her under the mistletoe and kissed her. It had been a very brief kiss, but then Olivia and her brother, Charles, had been looking on.

"And what has brought that beautiful pink blush to your cheeks, Miss Renwick?" Lord Felbridge's silky, deep voice interrupted her reminiscence.

Cassandra felt her face grow warm. "Oh! Nothing!

Nothing at all." She laughed self-consciously. "I am just enjoying the evening, my lord."

"Ah, I am very happy to hear that. And here I was afraid that you would be bored, just sitting here watching the dancing."

Mr. Saunders had returned with Lord Felbridge and had been talking quietly with Olivia. Now the two stood up.

"If you will excuse us, Miss Renwick, Fell, we are going to dance," Mr. Saunders said, taking Olivia's hand and escorting her from their box.

Lord Felbridge took Olivia's vacated seat, and Cassandra smoothed down her dress once again.

There was an awkward silence for a moment, as Cassandra searched her mind for something polite to say. Even after eight years of being taught proper deportment at school, she still found it difficult to start a conversation with a gentleman.

Lord Felbridge was looking at her somewhat speculatively, in a way that made her just a bit uncomfortable. He had a half smile on his face, as if he knew exactly the turmoil that was going on inside her.

They had already thoroughly discussed the weather. And the delights of Lady Broughton's soiree had also been well-digested earlier, together with the light repast of shaved ham for which Vauxhall was famous.

"Do you plan on attending the races at Haymarket next weekend?" she blurted out. She immediately realized that such a question from a young lady was quite inappropriate. She was not supposed to know of such things, or at least not take an interest in them.

"Cousin Charles has been talking about it nonstop for the past few days," she put in hastily.

Lord Felbridge quickly schooled his face into impassivity. She couldn't quite tell whether he had been shocked or amused that she had asked.

"Er, yes. I plan on driving down with Bradmore."

This was when Cassandra noticed the two ladies in the

box directly across from her. They had been staring at her ever since Lord Felbridge had sat down. But now they had their heads together, whispering something while stealing glances over toward her.

Cassandra smiled a little to herself. They were probably talking about what a handsome couple she and Lord Felbridge made.

She turned her bright smile on to her companion. He really was absolutely perfect for her. Tall and blond just as she was, although his eyes were a velvety brown while hers were blue. He was always impeccably dressed in the first stare of fashion, and she assured herself that she was certain to do likewise. Did she not have another appointment with her modiste just the following day?

Yes, the two ladies across from her were probably commenting on how very lucky Cassandra was to have caught one of the most eligible young men of the *ton.*

"Miss Renwick, would you care to go for a stroll about the gardens?" Lord Felbridge asked, interrupting her musing.

Cassandra's breath caught in her throat. This was it! Maybe he was going to propose after all! She took a deep breath to calm herself. She did not want to sound overly enthusiastic.

A proper young lady is never too enthusiastic. She must remain calm and poised at all times. The words of her school's headmistress sounded in her ears.

"That sounds lovely, my lord, thank you." Demurely, she placed her hand in his outstretched one and allowed him to lead her from their box.

"It is so romantic here!" Cassandra could not help herself. The twinkling of the colored lanterns in the trees, the soft music coming from somewhere just beyond the path, and the moonlit night all combined to create an atmosphere of festivity and romance. This was Vauxhall Gardens at its best.

A deep chuckle answered her enthusiasm. "Yes, they work very hard to create this aura of romance. And they do rather a good job of it too . . . if you are in the mood to succumb to it."

Lord Felbridge leaned closer to Cassandra. She could smell the wonderful musky scent of his cologne. As his lips brushed against her hair, he whispered softly in her ear, "Are you in the mood, Miss Renwick?"

Cassandra shivered, but could not restrain her embarrassed giggles. Oh, yes, she certainly was in the mood, especially with Lord Felbridge so close to her. She stole a quick glance up at him and then leaned a little closer on his arm, but retained her modesty by saying nothing.

The music and sounds of the more populated area of the gardens faded softly as they moved ever closer to the wooded pathways for which Vauxhall was so well known.

"Have I told you how lovely you look tonight, Miss Renwick?" Lord Felbridge asked quietly.

"Not as yet, my lord," Cassandra answered saucily, becoming bolder as they gained more privacy.

Lord Felbridge laughed. "Well, then, I have been horribly remiss, haven't I? Please do accept my humble apologies and know that I believe you to be one of the most beautiful girls here."

"Oh, now you are coming on too strong, my lord," Cassandra giggled.

"No, indeed. I am absolutely serious."

"Felbridge! Is that you?" A gentleman stopped in the near darkness directly in front of them.

Lord Felbridge and Cassandra stopped walking.

"Yes?" Lord Felbridge reached out and shook the man's hand. "Harkins! What a pleasant surprise! Haven't seen you in ages. Been rusticating?"

Cassandra suddenly felt as if she had been completely forgotten. But then Lord Felbridge turned to her and said, "Miss Renwick, this is my very good friend, the Earl of Harkins."

Lord Harkins bowed over her hand. "How do you do?"

Lord Felbridge grasped his friend's arm and began

walking back the way they had come. "If you will excuse us for just a moment, Miss Renwick. I have some urgent business with Lord Harkins. But, I promise you, I won't be more than a minute."

Cassandra was shocked as she watched the two men walk around the corner and out of sight. She was being left alone on a dark pathway while her escort chatted with his friend? She had always thought Lord Felbridge to have the most perfect manners.

A minute passed by while Cassandra stood alone in the dark. She shivered, her annoyance dissipating while mild apprehension overtook her. Vauxhall Gardens was full of people, she told herself. She was in no danger at all. Yet, being alone at night in a near forest was rather frightening, despite the faint sounds of laughter and the mumble of voices and music from so far away.

Perhaps, Cassandra thought, she could move to where she could at least see the two men. And surely their brief business discussion was over by now.

As she had expected, the two gentlemen were not far. She smiled as she caught the last words from Lord Harkins. Their business was, indeed, concluded.

"Then that's settled, Felly. A hundred guineas on Waving Wind."

The men shook hands, and were about to part, when Lord Harkins turned back.

"Now tell me this, Felly, my boy, who is this chit? Never heard of the Renwicks."

Cassandra shrank into the shadows, eager to hear the rest, but knowing full well that she shouldn't.

Lord Felbridge laughed briefly. "Oh, she is a nobody I am amusing myself with. Of no importance whatsoever, I assure you. You in town for long? You must come and see this new gaming hell that has opened up. It is quite good. I won six hundred off of Barnslow last night."

"Count me in, my friend. See you there about one?"

"Oh no, I'll be there much before that. Another fifteen minutes of making love to this girl and I will be bored beyond belief. Besides, she is a proper young miss, so I'm not likely to get very far. I'll try my luck, but otherwise I should be at the club before too long."

His friend smiled broadly at Felbridge, his shoulders shaking with suppressed laughter.

"You're always a card, Felly!"

"Am I? Well, you have yet to hear the really amusing part." Felbridge paused, his voice shaking with laughter. "She thinks she may actually have a chance of getting *me* into the parson's mousetrap! As if I would even consider the daughter of a baronet. It is utterly ridiculous! You should have seen Sefton's face when I told him. He was hysterical with laughter—in fact most of the fellows at the club were."

Harkins gave up his fight to suppress his laughter. As his chuckles subsided, he patted Lord Felbridge on the back. "Enjoy your game. Until later, then."

Cassandra quickly jumped back to where she had been left. He had told the other gentlemen at his club and had a good laugh about her? That meant that rumors were already spreading through every drawing room of the *ton*.

She was ruined!

How could he have done this to her? Cassandra bit her lip to hold back her tears.

Lord Felbridge, still smiling when he rejoined her, deftly put his arm around her waist. "Now where were we? Ah yes, I was saying how lovely you look this evening, was I not?"

Surreptitiously wiping at her wet cheeks with her hand, Cassandra was grateful for the darkness. She would not let this incredibly rude and horrible man see how upset she was. That would not do.

"If you do not mind, my lord, I would like to go back to the table," she said as calmly as possible while moving away from him.

I do not want to bore you any more than I already have, she added silently to herself. *Nor do I want to provide any more fodder for the ever-hungry gossips of the ton.* She longed to let this thoughtless, haughty man know that she had overheard him. But, of course, that would only increase his amusement. So it was not even worth wasting her breath.

"Oh come now, Miss Renwick," Lord Felbridge said, taking hold of her hand. "You are not upset because I stopped for a moment to speak with an old friend, are you?"

"No, of course not . . ."

"No, you are much too knowledgeable in the ways of society for that."

Now he was laughing at her! She was sure of it.

"My dear Cassandra, come now, give me a kiss and say you'll forgive me?"

Cassandra was shocked! He wanted her to kiss him? She would sooner kiss a toad! She looked around her for a good way to get out of this, but was chagrined to see that he had led her into one of the dark alcoves. There was no one in sight.

He moved closer, putting his hand on the small of her back to make sure she couldn't run away.

"P-please, Lord Felbridge. I would rather you took me back to my cousin." She put her hands on his chest to stop him from coming any closer, but already it was almost too late. She turned her head away as he bent toward her, ready to press his lips to hers. "Please, my lord! Don't make me scream for help."

Lord Felbridge froze where he was, less than an inch from her face. Then he straightened up and shrugged. "Very well, if that is the way you feel. I thought that you had warmer sentiments toward me than that. But if you wish to go, then, by all means, let us return to your cousin immediately."

He took a step back and then once again held out his arm for her to take, as if nothing had happened.

Upset as she was, she contemplated not taking it. But that would not do. It would not do to show the world how she was feeling. She had been taught well at school. She took a deep breath, straightened her back and took Lord Felbridge's arm.

When they reached their box, she sat down next to Olivia while the gentlemen stood behind them and talked quietly together.

"Well?" Olivia whispered, leaning close.

"I want to leave, Olivia," Cassandra whispered back. "I want to leave Vauxhall Gardens. I want to leave London. I want to leave England altogether." She paused in thought for a moment.

"I want to go to my parents in Calcutta."

1

Julian Ritchie entered the ballroom with his usual self-confident swagger. This night was going to be different, he told himself.

He didn't know what it was that made him think so. Indeed, he had entered many a ballroom before thinking the very same thing, only to be severely disappointed.

But tonight there was something in the air—something magical. It was going to be a good night.

He stopped for a moment just inside the door and took in the ballroom. The brilliant colors of the ladies' dresses and the officers' uniforms warred with the vibrant colors of the flowers which were everywhere, overflowing from sconces on the walls and in vases on every surface. The smell filled the room. It made for a very nice change from the street smell of spices and animals that always seemed to hang in the air.

And then there were the people themselves. All of Calcutta's English society was here. Everyone who was anyone had been invited to Miss Renwick's coming-out ball. He could even see a few prominent, wealthy Indian gentlemen present.

Julian had been a little surprised that he had been invited, but then, everyone in his office had been on the list of invitees. It would have been too obvious a cut if he alone had been left out.

Besides, he believed his employer, Sir Lionel Renwick, rather liked him, despite the fact that his wife loathed the sight of him. He suspected that Sir Lionel had insisted on Julian receiving an invitation. Lady Renwick certainly would not have issued one otherwise.

Julian took a deep breath and headed for the first group of people who were standing and chatting nearest the door.

"How do you do, Mrs. Hurst, Miss Hurst," Julian said, bowing to the two ladies.

Adelaide Hurst turned around, gave an imperious sniff and then turned her back on him once again. Her daughter, Anne, did little better, managing a small nod in his direction before turning back to her conversation.

Julian did not let their reactions bother him. He moved on, slowly strolling about the room and nodding to people who deigned to notice his existence.

He stopped outside a few different groups of people whom he knew, but they always closed their ranks against him just as he approached.

He found Sir Lionel in conversation with Lord Minto.

"Good evening, sirs," Julian said, bowing to them.

"Ah, Ritchie," Sir Lionel said, nodding to him, "I am happy to see you could make it."

"Good evening, Ritchie." Lord Minto gave him a very brief smile and then turned back to his conversation with Sir Lionel.

Well, it was the warmest welcome he had received all evening, Julian reasoned.

He turned toward the dance floor. The dancers hopped and skipped about as they executed the complicated steps of an English country dance.

But his gaze was held captive by the young woman at the head of the line. She was dressed in white and staring directly at him.

Julian could not help himself. He stared right back.
She was beautiful.

Julian felt an odd sensation in his stomach. A fire had
been lit somewhere inside of him. Heat rushed through
him as he watched her.

She was like a porcelain doll. Her creamy complexion
was set off by just a little flush of color on her cheeks
from the exertion of the dance. Her eyes were the color
of the sky and her hair the color of the sun.

If her mouth was a little too wide, or her nose a little
too small, he could not say. To him, she was perfect.

But why was she looking at him, of all people?

Cassandra could not imagine why her eyes kept straying toward the man in the old-fashioned blue coat. That
he was unusually handsome and stood out from the
other gentlemen present did not weigh with her. She was
not interested in men. Not any more. Not after what
Lord Felbridge had done to her.

And yet her eyes kept finding their way to him.

Cassandra studied the man. What was it about him
that made him stand out so? Yes, he was tall and his high
cheekbones and strong jaw were exceptionally pleasing
to the eye.

His eyes were the most amazing color. They were not
quite green and yet not quite blue, but something in
between—turquoise, she supposed.

Although the cut of his coat was out of date, it was well-
cut and it was easy to see that he had a fine physique. And
he looked like he had been out in the sun too long, his
skin was so brown—clearly he did something that involved
some work outdoors. Perhaps some sport, since he was
clearly a gentleman?

But there was more to him than merely his physical at-
tractiveness. He had something elusive, a presence that
drew her eyes and her attention.

Something that made everyone else in the room seem insignificant.

That was bad.

She was supposed to be paying attention to Major Vernon, her dance partner for the fourth time this evening. But she simply could not garner up any enthusiasm for the ruddy-cheeked major—who, with his fulsome attentions, was reminding her of all the other cads she had met since that fateful day in Vauxhall.

"You look very serious, Miss Renwick," Major Vernon said, smiling, yet looking at her with narrowed eyes.

"Oh! I am so sorry, Major. My mind was wandering, I'm afraid."

He looked hurt. Cassandra couldn't imagine why—it wasn't as if he was providing scintillating conversation to distract her.

She suppressed a sigh and then tried to think of something to say.

"Do you go out often, Major? To parties and such?" she asked.

"Whenever I can, Miss Renwick. Do you enjoy parties?"

Cassandra thought about that for a moment. She used to enjoy going to parties very much when she first arrived in London. But then came Lord Felbridge to destroy that joy for her. Now she truly had no desire to be out in company, but she supposed she should not say as much.

"I enjoy dancing very much." That, at least, was the truth.

"And you are an excellent dancer," he said, just before they moved away from each other.

Cassandra's eyes wandered over to the gentleman in the blue coat, and then widened in astonishment. Had Miss Stroughton just given him the cut direct?

Cassandra had to turn about with the movements of the dance, but she could have sworn he was being treated in the most monstrous way. When she caught sight of him once again, he had moved to another group of people, a smile plastered to his face as yet another person turned her back to him.

Cassandra had to fight the urge to run to his side. She wished she could do something to stop this horrific behavior! How could people behave this way?

Unexpectedly, she felt tears sting her eyes.

"You are still looking very upset, Miss Renwick." Major Vernon's voice reclaimed her attention.

She turned to him, this time completely unable to muster up even a smile. "I am so sorry, Major. I was just wondering if you knew that man over there. I believe he has just been given the cut direct, and I've noticed that very few people seem to be speaking to him. Has he done something horribly gauche?"

The Major looked over his shoulder. When he turned back to her, his eyebrows were drawn down and he looked very displeased. "You too should have nothing to do with that man. He is a nobody."

Cassandra drew a sharp breath and fought to keep herself from slapping Major Vernon's smiling, superior-looking face. Lord Felbridge's words were echoing in her mind.

He had called her a nobody as well.

"That is a horrible thing to say! How dare you? Everybody is somebody. And I'd like to know who that man is," she said hotly.

"I am terribly sorry if I have hurt your delicate sensibilities, Miss Renwick. It is very good of you to think that way, but truly, you should have nothing to do with that man. I am surprised he was even invited this evening. As you noted, no one is speaking with him. He has no place among us."

He tightened his grip on Cassandra's hand. "If I were you, Miss Renwick, I would stay away from Julian Ritchie."

"Mother!" Cassandra whispered fiercely. She could not believe how embarrassing this was. She simply was not going to dance with Major Vernon yet again! "Mother, this is unseemly! In London if one dances with a gentleman more than twice, you are as good as engaged."

Her mother smiled and nodded. "That is in London, my dear. We are in Calcutta, and I am certain that the major does not mind, do you, sir?"

Major Vernon smiled brightly at Cassandra. "Not at all. It is an honor and a pleasure to dance with such a lovely young lady."

Cassandra just could not find it in her to return his smile. She knew she should, but she was tired.

In fact, she had not even wanted to have this ball in the first place. She had argued with her mother about it for a while, but in the end had allowed her mother to win. Lady Renwick had been so upset at the thought that Cassandra had not wanted a coming-out ball that Cassandra just could not break her heart.

But this time, her mother would not win. She simply would *not* dance with Major Vernon yet again.

"I am very sorry, Major, but I simply cannot dance with you again. Mama, I am going to get some refreshment, and look, Mrs. Hurst is trying to get your attention."

Julian stood at the refreshment table, helping himself to a lobster patty. A tap on his shoulder made him turn around to see his best friend, Reginald White.

"Don't eat too many of those or you might end up like me," Reggie said, smiling broadly and patting his round belly.

"Have no fear, Reggie. I don't believe I will ever be as, er, comfortable as you are." Julian laughed. "I haven't seen you dancing as yet."

"Oh, I shall. I shall. Just have to find the right girl, you know."

"Ah yes, a particular young Miss Blighten, no?"

His friend's complexion went from its usual light pink to a much deeper shade of the color. "Yes, well . . ."

"If you wait much longer, you shall have to follow my lead."

"Oh?"

"Yes. I am going to ask a young lady to dance," Julian said. He looked about the room once more, but was brought up short to see Miss Renwick walking directly toward him. He had planned on asking her dance, but here she was approaching him!

"Julian," Reggie said warningly.

"Do not worry, Reggie. I am simply going to follow up on a certain look which I received from the young lady—or should I say, looks. And do not look now, but here she is."

As Reggie whipped around, Julian quickly wiped his greasy fingers on his handkerchief and pulled on his white gloves. He had the pleasure of seeing his friend's jaw literally drop at the sight of his quarry.

Reggie quickly recovered himself just as the young lady joined them. "Good evening, Miss Renwick," he said, bowing to her.

"Good evening, Mr. White. I hope you are enjoying yourself?"

"Y-yes. Yes, indeed, thank you."

"Miss Renwick, may I be so bold as to introduce myself?" Julian said, nearly cutting off his friend.

Miss Renwick gave him an encouraging smile.

"I am Julian Ritchie, one of your father's clerks."

"I am pleased to meet you, Mr. Ritchie," she said softly.

Julian felt his stomach tighten. Had he ever met such a sweet young lady? He rather thought not.

He took a deep breath and steeled himself for the usual stab of rejection. "Miss Renwick, would you care to dance?"

"I would be delighted, sir." She held her hand out for him to take.

Julian could not help but give both Miss Renwick and Reggie a broad smile.

From either side of them, Julian could hear gasps of

outrage as they took their places for a country dance. But Julian ignored them, and, he was pleased to see, so did Miss Renwick.

Instead, she smiled even more brightly up at him. She curtseyed to him in the most graceful way as the orchestra began to play.

Murmurs, exclamations and shock followed them throughout the dance, but Julian held his head up high and continued to smile at Miss Renwick. He did not know why she continued to ignore the comments, but he was incredibly grateful that she did.

After a short time, the sounds all around them seemed to fade away. All he could hear were the sweet strains of the music and all he felt were her hands in his own.

She moved so gracefully. Julian found himself completely unable to take his eyes from her. Perhaps it was just wishful thinking, but he thought that she had not taken her eyes from him either.

Julian called himself to order. They could not just stare at each other through the entire dance. He had to make some sort of conversation. He gave her a smile.

"I am certain everyone has asked you already, but how are you adapting to Calcutta? I have heard that it is quite a change from London."

"Do you know, you are the first person to ask me how I am doing?" she said, with a sparkle in her eye and the most lovely little smile. They moved apart with the movements of the dance.

When they were brought back together again, she said, "The people I've met so far only want to hear news from home and are not so interested in how I am coping with the change."

He moved around the lady next to him as they advanced through the dance.

"So how have you been coping?" he asked when they were back together again.

"Quite well, actually, thank you. It is not as hot as I had expected."

"But it is winter. Just wait until April and you will be wishing yourself anywhere but here."

She laughed, but could not give him a rejoinder as the dance had moved them apart once again.

Julian noticed the whispers and stares once more as he led another young lady round about in a circle. He wondered what Miss Renwick must be thinking of all this. How was it that she was not bothered by them?

It was clear, by contrast, that the young lady he was with was not happy with him as her partner for the moment—she was frowning fiercely at him and her face was uncommonly flushed.

He was grateful to return to Miss Renwick's smiling countenance and easy acceptance of him. She seemed to be truly enjoying his company and was somehow able to completely ignore everything else that was going on around them.

"Well, I am enjoying being here so far, and I suppose I will just have to learn to deal with the heat as everyone else does."

"That would be by escaping it. We all travel to the mountains when it gets too warm. To the hill stations."

"Oh yes? I have so much to learn. It is all very exciting and quite fascinating," she said, curtseying to him.

As the dance had ended on that note, Julian was not given an opportunity to respond to Miss Renwick's enthusiasm. But with her obvious indifference to society and its rules and her interest in Calcutta, an idea was beginning to germinate in Julian's mind.

He would have to think on it, though. It wasn't something that one just jumped into with both feet. Not like taking the chance and asking Sir Lionel's daughter to dance.

But he might just do anything to be with Miss Renwick again.

Julian set aside his thoughts as he led Miss Renwick back to her parents. Lady Renwick looked like she had swallowed a lemon and the veins in her neck were standing out—definitely not a good sign.

He bowed once more to the young lady. "I must thank you, Miss Renwick, for a most enjoyable dance. I am deeply honored. . . ."

"And so you should be," Lady Renwick interrupted, frowning at him fiercely.

"I thank you, sir, for the dance," Miss Renwick quickly put in. "You are an excellent dancer. I hope I have an opportunity to meet you again sometime soon."

"Not if I can help it," Lady Renwick said, with a quick glance to her husband for support. He had looked away at that moment, and completely missed what she had said.

Julian dared to look at Miss Renwick to see if she mirrored her mother's sentiments. Instead, a look of sympathy flashed in her eyes, and Julian had the oddest feeling that she knew exactly what he was going through just at this moment.

But how could that be? How could such an incredibly beautiful young English woman know what it was like to be an outcast, to be shunned by society?

It was impossible. Yet the sympathy and understanding she showed him sent waves of warmth through his body, right down to his toes.

2

It was nearly midnight, but Julian wasn't quite ready to go home. And he was intrigued by Reggie's behavior. He had been eyeing Julian nervously for much of the evening.

"All right, out with it, old man," he said, leaning forward on the slightly worn brown sofa that graced Reggie's drawing room.

"No, no, it is nothing." Reggie stopped and wrung his pudgy hands together.

"You could never hide things from me, Reggie. I've known you for much too long. You have been as nervous as a cat all evening."

"Have I?" Reggie's voice was abnormally high.

"Yes, and if you don't tell me what it is right now . . ." Julian gave his friend a teasing smile and started to rise from the sofa to come toward him.

"I got the promotion," Reggie spat out quickly.

Julian stopped abruptly. The smile slipped off his face as he sat back down.

"It wasn't me. I mean . . . I didn't ask for it . . ." Reggie's voice trailed off. "Julian?"

Julian sat back, feeling the heat of anger seep into his stomach. It was almost pleasing, the flame of rage that licked at him. Julian wanted so much to let it burst out and lash out at the furniture, at Reggie. . . .

But Reggie did not deserve that. It took a great deal of effort, but Julian turned his lips up into a smile. Moving a bit slower than usual, he reached out to pat his friend on the back. "That is wonderful, Reggie, I am really happy for you. Congratulations!"

Reggie sighed with relief and gave a nervous little laugh. "It should have been you. We all know that, Julian."

"No, no. You have worked very hard for this promotion and you deserve it. We'll celebrate. Yes, that is just what we need to do. Let us get a bottle of the best wine and drink a toast to you and your success!"

His friend blushed. "Thank you. Thank you, Julian, you *are* a good friend."

Julian gave Reggie a smile. Then he got up from the sofa and called to Reggie's servant. He quickly gave him orders and then slipped him a tip before turning back to his friend.

"So that was why Sir Lionel called you into his office today—to tell you the good news," Julian said, sitting back down.

"Yes. He said that my work for the past year has been exemplary and he felt that I deserved the promotion."

"And so you do," Julian concurred.

"But you have been there for over two years, Julian. Why, you taught me everything I know. I can't imagine why he did not give the promotion to you."

The servant came back bearing a tray with a bottle of wine and two glasses. Julian got up and took it from him, dismissing him with a nod of his head. He opened the bottle and poured the deep red liquid into the glasses.

"Here's to you and your fine work," he said, raising his glass.

Reggie blushed again, but acknowledged his friend's salute gracefully.

Julian drank deeply, nearly finishing the entire glass at

once. He wished it were something stronger, but took what solace he could from the wine.

He refilled his glass and Reggie's and then raised it again. "And here is to Sir Lionel, may he grow a backbone—in order to stand up to the bigots of the world before I die of old age in my current position."

This glass he finished completely, but then noticed that Reggie had not drunk any of his own.

"Do you think it was prejudice that made him promote me instead of you?" his friend asked quietly.

"Not Sir Lionel's prejudice perhaps, but that of innumerable others I could name. If only . . . well, you have worked very hard, Reggie, and you *do* deserve to be promoted. But you are not the first to be promoted from below me, and you are certainly not going to be the last," Julian said, sitting down heavily on the sofa.

"Sir Lionel simply will never have the nerve to promote an Indian, no matter what," he said, reaching forward once more to refill his glass.

"But you are not wholly Indian. Your father was English."

Julian shook his head. "If you think that matters one whit, you are fooling yourself. Even if both of my parents and all my grandparents were English and only my great-great-grandfather were Indian, I would still be considered a native and therefore not worth the mud on Lady Renwick's half-boots."

"No, Julian, that can't be true!" Reggie cried, truly distressed.

"Yes, my friend, it is indeed true," Julian said, giving him a small, rueful smile.

But then his brow cleared and he gave Reggie a true smile. "However, I may have a plan." He drained his glass again.

"A plan? What sort of plan?" Reggie asked nervously.

"I shall not tell you, my friend. It needs a little more thinking through. But I assure you, when the time is right, I will do what a man should do."

"Julian, what are you thinking? Please do not do anything stupid," Reggie pleaded.

He smiled and patted Reggie's rounded and flushed cheek. "Have no fear, Reggie. You will know all in good time. I would not leave you out in the cold."

Reggie was scared. Julian could see it in his eyes, but he did not care. Julian Ritchie may have been overlooked for promotion twice, he may have needed to ignore the constant slights and insults heaped upon him by Lady Renwick and other Englishmen both within the government and without for the past two years, but he would stand for it no longer. It was time for him to act like the man he knew he was.

There was only so much intolerance a man could take, and Julian had just reached his limit.

Cassandra awoke with a start. She sat up, aware of a movement behind her, and turned to see a small lizard scurrying up the wall—a flash of green in a patch of morning light streaming in through the window.

She stifled a scream and then remembered that these creatures were harmless to people and kept the multitude of Indian insects at bay.

Cassandra stretched languorously, a knot of determination forming in her mind. Today she would not allow her mother to force her to go out and pay social calls.

She had done her duty. She had been kind and charming to all of the men she had been forced to dance with the previous evening, including the ever-present Major Vernon. She had remembered all of the ladies' names and chatted with them amiably.

Now she just wanted to be left alone.

Cassandra attempted to get up, but was held back by the mosquito netting that surrounded her bed. She tried to untuck an edge from under the mattress, but found it surprisingly difficult to do so while still on the bed. Just as she was beginning to feel mildly claustrophobic, her new maid, Gita, came in and hurried over to help.

"Your mother is waiting for you on the veranda, Miss," she said as she tucked the mosquito net up and out of the way.

Cassandra got up and picked out the plainest gown she owned from her wardrobe.

"Perhaps you would like to wear your new blue-striped muslin?" Gita asked softly. "You look so lovely in it."

Cassandra stopped and looked at Gita, who smiled encouragingly at her with her head tilted to the side just a little. Cassandra was quickly learning that this was a very Indian gesture—it was both submissive and yet determined.

"No. I am going to wear this. I will not be going out today."

"My lady has asked me to see that you are properly dressed, Miss. I am certain that she means for you to be going out."

"She may mean for me to go out, but I shall not."

Enough was enough. She had played along with her mother's plans since she had arrived, simply because her mother had been so excited by her arrival.

But no longer. She had been here long enough and done enough. Now she was going to do what she wanted.

Her maid closed her eyes for a moment in resignation and helped Cassandra into her dress.

As Cassandra left her room, she nearly tripped over the two tailors who had been sitting in the hall silently stitching her new dresses. They immediately jumped up to salaam her as she passed by.

Even though she had been in Calcutta for a little more than two weeks, she still marveled at how different things were compared to the pristine and cool cleanliness of Miss Stillwater's School for Girls.

Everything here was slightly dusty, she thought to herself as she made her way down the hall. The dust lightly floured every surface—despite the fact that the shutters were kept closed for most of the day and the sweeper came through twice a day with his brooms, gathering piles of dust as he moved silently through each room.

As she neared the entrance to the veranda, Cassandra once again nearly tripped over another servant. This time it was the punkha-wallah—the man who pulled the cord that waved a large fan on the veranda back and forth. On the veranda itself, four servants stood against the wall, seemingly doing nothing.

She stepped into the pleasantly informal sunroom. It was already awash with bright sunlight and filled with the lovely smell of flowers, which came in from the garden just below through the large open windows.

"There are so many servants about, Mama. Are you certain that you need them all?" she asked, as yet another liveried servant held out a chair for her at the table.

"You will get used to them, my dear. Why, I do not even see them anymore. They are like pieces of furniture." Lady Renwick waved her hand dismissively.

"Oh no, Mother, really!" Cassandra cried, horrified at the callously dismissive comment.

"Yes, really, Cassandra. Well, what can you expect when, as you say, there are so many of them around? I am not even sure what some of them do," her mother said, idly taking a sip of her tea.

"How can you not know what people in your own house do? Do you not keep track of all that?" Cassandra quickly sat down in her chair, after realizing that the servant holding it was not going to move until she did so.

"No, that is the job of the bania. He runs the house, hires and fires all the servants, and is responsible for them."

Cassandra was taken aback at discovering this aspect of her mother, who, she was realizing, was somewhat of a stranger to her. In England, the precision and efficiency with which Lady Renwick ran her household had been well known throughout their locality. Surely that had not been entirely the work of her housekeeper?

Now, Cassandra began to wonder.

A server materialized at her elbow, presenting a platter heaped with familiar English food. She helped herself to some toast and a fried egg. Tea was poured for her before she had even had time to request it, and the server disappeared into the background as noiselessly as he had appeared.

"Speaking of which, I suppose I shall have to inform the bania to find another ayah for you. Clearly this one cannot carry out her instructions."

"What do you mean, Mama? I like Gita very much."

"Perhaps, but I told her that you were to be dressed properly and I see that you are not. That gown should be thrown out."

"I like this gown! And it is not Gita's fault that I am dressed in it. She wanted me to wear my new blue dress, but I refused."

Cassandra took a deep breath and lifted her chin a notch. "Mama, I will not be going out visiting with you today."

"Do not be ridiculous, Cassandra. Of course you will be going out visiting. And not only that, but I am certain that you will have quite a few gentleman callers."

Cassandra carefully buttered her toast. "I shall not be receiving them."

"I beg your pardon?" her mother's lips thinned in displeasure.

"I would not want to falsely encourage anyone," she said, taking a bite.

Her mother sat in silence watching her eat, the veins in her neck beginning to stand out as they did whenever she was angry. She then sat back in her chair. "All right, Cassandra, enough playing games. I believe it is time you told me exactly why you are here in Calcutta."

Cassandra blinked, her fork suspended in mid-air. She swallowed the mouthful of egg she had just taken and hurriedly took a sip of her tea. "I'm sorry, Mama, what do you mean? I am here to be with you and Papa, of course. My schooling is finished." Her practiced lie slid smoothly from her lips.

Her mother frowned at her. "Do please give me some credit, my dear, for being more intelligent than that."

"Mama!"

"You were to be presented by Cousin Amelia. To make your come-out with Olivia. What happened to change those plans?"

Cassandra sat back and folded her hands around the napkin in her lap, fidgeting with the cloth. Should she? Could she tell her mother the truth? Would she too laugh at her as all of society had done? Would she be hurt by the slight to her own prestige?

Cassandra looked at her mother and tried to determine what she should do.

Her mother reached out and stilled Cassandra's hands. "Cassandra, I am your mother. You may tell me anything."

"It, it didn't work out." Cassandra gave a little shrug of her shoulders and tried to smile. All of her hurt, all of her pain came flooding back in her mother's simple gesture. She fought to breathe around the lump that had formed in her throat.

"What do you mean? You did not give it much of a chance from what I understand. You came down from school at the end of May, spent the month of June in London and were on the ship to India by July. One month does not make a season, Cassandra. It barely gives you time at all to attend any parties or balls. Now tell me, what really happened?"

Cassandra looked at her mother. She hadn't been entirely sure what to expect of a mother whom she had not seen in eight years, but it certainly wasn't this direct, hard woman. In fact, from her letters, Cassandra assumed that she would be a rather frivolous, carefree sort of person who never really gave much of a thought to anything beyond the next social event and who her daughter would marry.

But now, of course, Cassandra was trapped. She had to

tell her mother the truth. There could be no getting around it.

Cassandra swallowed her pain. Surely her own mother would not blame her? She carefully folded the napkin on her lap and set it next to her plate of forgotten food.

She wasn't entirely sure how to begin. The whole thing was so embarrassing. But her mother was waiting.

Cassandra continued to fiddle with the napkin as she tried to formulate her thoughts.

Lady Renwick sighed and stilled her daughter's hands once again. She said, "Come now, Cassandra, you can tell me. Was it your cousin, Olivia? Did the two of you not get along? I am certain that she could not outshine you. If I remember correctly, she was a rather mousy little girl with brown hair and eyes."

"Oh no, Mama. Olivia is wonderful. She is my closest friend, and brown hair and eyes are all the rage, I assure you."

Her mother nodded skeptically. "Well then?"

Cassandra took a deep, wavering breath. "I . . . I fell in love, Mama."

Her mother's eyes went wide. "With whom?"

Cassandra turned her face to the garden and then proceeded to tell her mother all about Lord Felbridge and what had happened that fateful night at Vauxhall Gardens—the worst night of her life.

"Then what?" her mother prodded gently.

"Then all of society began laughing at me. They called me a cheeky little thing—for it was obvious to everyone that Lord Felbridge would never stoop so low as to marry the daughter of a mere baronet."

Cassandra sat silently looking out at the garden. A small green lizard scuttled along the window sill, snatched a beautiful yellow butterfly from the air with its mouth and then quickly disappeared out of sight again.

She looked away, back toward her mother. Her mother had not said anything, but once again the long ropes of veins in her neck stood out.

Slowly, Cassandra went on, "Mama, they did not care that Papa held an extremely important position in India, nor that I was cousin to an earl. They only cared that Lord Felbridge found it amusing to . . . to lead me on and then to laugh at me."

A servant approached the table cautiously. A nod from Lady Renwick, and he quickly cleared away the breakfast dishes.

Cassandra sighed deeply as the man left. "I was thoroughly humiliated, Mama. People began to cut me. I could not bear it. I worried that it was damaging Olivia's reputation as well, because we were always together. I just couldn't allow that to happen.

"I just could not hurt Olivia's chances as well. So I left."

Cassandra hastily wiped away at the tears that had started to slip down her cheeks. "It was unbearable. I could go nowhere without people laughing at me behind my back. I saw them whispering behind their hands. . . ." She let out a little sob and buried her face in her napkin.

"People can be very cruel, Cassandra. It is always a hard lesson to learn. However, it is clear that you did not handle the situation correctly either. Had I been there to guide you, I assure you, it would have turned out differently."

Her mother sniffed and looked toward the garden. "I am surprised that Cousin Amelia did not see to your reputation. She could have nipped that gossip in the bud had she wanted to, I am sure."

"I don't know, Mama. I'm sure that she spoke up in my defense. . . ."

"Well, clearly not strongly enough." She motioned for her teacup to be refilled by one of the servants who stood along the wall.

"However, you are here now and I will see to you. All shall be well, Cassandra," she said, adding some milk to her tea. "You shall marry Major Vernon. He is a very good man from a good family and is well on his way to a superior position here."

"But Mama, I don't want to marry Major Vernon. I don't want to marry anyone. I don't want to go out into society, I . . ."

"Then what do you want to do, Cassandra?" her mother snapped.

Cassandra stopped. "I . . . I don't know. I just want to be left alone."

"To do what? You are not independently wealthy, Cassandra. You do not have the money to become an eccentric old maid. Do you want to become companion to some crotchety old woman? Do you want to become governess to someone else's brats? Those are your only options."

Cassandra was quiet. She didn't know what she wanted. She didn't know what she was going to do. All she knew was that men could not be trusted and right now she did not want to have anything to do with them.

"I am not ready, Mama," she said.

"Ready or not, Cassandra, you are of age to marry and you *will* marry." Her mother's voice was firm, her edict final.

They sat glaring stubbornly at each other for a moment. Her mother was the first to blink. She softened her eyes, saying, "I am sure that Major Vernon will put that horrid Lord Felbridge right out of your mind."

Cassandra watched her mother sip at her tea.

The only man who had ever successfully put Lord Felbridge out of her mind was Julian Ritchie. The way he had been treated the night before made her heart go out to him. He was someone who would understand what she had been through.

She certainly didn't want to marry him, but if all her mother was looking for was someone to rid her mind of Lord Felbridge . . .

"What about Mr. Ritchie? He is a very kind . . ." Cassandra stopped speaking. The veins in her mother's neck began to stand out once again and her lips pinched together.

"Do not even think of him. He is far beneath your

notice. Just because he danced with you last night does not make him a suitable match for you."

"But . . ."

"Cassandra, you will listen to me."

Cassandra knew that she had better not say any more. She looked down at her hands clenched in her lap, but then looked her mother straight in the eye.

"Very well, Mother. But I will *not* marry Major Vernon."

3

Cassandra was gently admiring a vase filled with large red hibiscus flowers when her father came into the room. "Look, my dear, here is Julian come to pay his respects to our little Cassie."

Cassandra spun around so fast that she nearly lost her balance. Mr. Ritchie stood awkwardly just inside the door slightly behind her father.

He looked, if possible, even more handsome than he had last night. He was dressed neatly and carried off his slightly unfashionable clothes with unconscious flair. If his boots were not quite so dazzlingly shiny as they should have been, Cassandra did not care to notice.

"Cassandra is not a child any longer, so please do not address her as such," her mother said coldly to Sir Lionel.

"Er, yes, yes, of course. Keep forgetting," Sir Lionel said, now looking as awkward as Mr. Ritchie. However, he quickly regained his equilibrium and turned to present Mr. Ritchie.

"Er, Cassandra, you remember my clerk, Julian Ritchie?"

"Yes, of course. How do you do, sir?" Cassandra curtsied and smiled encouragingly.

"It is an honor, Miss Renwick," Mr. Ritchie said, bowing to her formally. He stole a glance at Cassandra's mother and then back, nervously holding a small package made up of a broad green leaf.

Lady Renwick could not have looked any less welcoming. Her mouth was pinched together and looked like she was physically holding back a scathing comment.

Cassandra's heart went out to him. She tried to smile reassuringly and tell him with her eyes that she welcomed him even if her mother did not.

He seemed to understand, for he took a deep breath and, with a quick glance at Lady Renwick, he stepped forward holding out the package toward Cassandra. "I, I brought these for you."

"Thank you," she said. She opened the leaf to find a handful of beautiful white flowers. "Oh, these are lovely!"

She picked one up and found that they were all attached by a string. As she lifted it, the smell of the flowers was released, wafting gently up to her. It was different from anything she had ever smelled before—sweet and spicy at the same time and utterly delicious.

Holding up the string of flowers, she said, "Do you wear them like a necklace?"

"Er, no. Ladies wear them in their hair." He paused and then stepped forward even closer. "If I may?"

He gently took the flowers from her hand and then moved behind her.

As he wound the flowers around the knot of hair at the top of her head, she could hear his heavy breathing and feel the heat emanating from his body. An overwhelming desire to close her eyes and lean backward toward him overcame her, but she held herself straight and away.

There was something about this man—he was tall and broad, not in a frightening way like Lord Felbridge, but in a comforting way, as if he could protect her from the world with a wave of his strong arm.

All too soon, he came back around to face her, standing a proper distance away. His color was slightly heightened and she supposed hers was as well.

"Thank you," she whispered, unable to make her voice work properly.

She wished she could move closer to him. It had been such a wonderful sensation being so near him, but the spell was abruptly broken when her father cleared his throat.

Cassandra blinked and suddenly became aware of everything around her again. How had she forgotten where she was, and goodness, that her parents were in the room?

"Sir Lionel, don't you and Mr. Ritchie have work to which you must attend?" her mother's voice sounded strained and clipped.

"Er, yes, well, that is, I do. Ritchie's day off, you know," her father said, and then quickly disappeared out the door without another word.

Mr. Ritchie's eyes opened wide at Sir Lionel's defection. His mouth opened as if he were going to say something, but Lady Renwick cut him off.

"Well, in that case, Mr. Ritchie, I am certain you have to be somewhere else?" she said pointedly.

Mr. Ritchie caught Cassandra's eye. She silently pleaded with him to stay, but tried to show that she would understand if he did not want to. Her mother, however, could not have been any less obvious in her dismissal.

His blue eyes seemed to apologize to her as he said, "Yes, I am afraid that I do need to go."

He paused and then a twinkle of mischief shone from his eyes. "I did, however, wish to be introduced to Miss Renwick . . . properly. It has been an honor."

With that he bowed to the ladies and left.

Cassandra wanted to laugh. Not only had he stood up to her mother, but he had very cleverly given her the stab of his anger. Perhaps he wasn't totally helpless after all.

Her mother, however, was clearly not pleased. "I told you, Cassandra, that man goes beyond the line of proper behavior. Putting flowers in your hair and being rude to his superiors!"

Yes, thought Cassandra to herself, *there is certainly much to be admired in Mr. Ritchie.*

Julian stopped just inside the door to his house. He removed his boots with a great deal of care, so as to not scratch them further. Placing them next to a few pairs of women's sandals, he walked down the hallway in his stockinged feet, humming a jaunty tune.

Entering the drawing room, he found his mother sitting with her back against a bolster on the thickly carpeted floor, savoring a cup of tea.

She looked up when he entered the room, and a broad smile spread over her beautiful round face. "Julian!"

"Good morning, Ma. Teatime already?" Julian greeted his mother in her native language, Bengali, and then bowed down to touch her feet in the traditional Indian greeting to elders.

She accepted her son's gesture by moving her feet so Julian could reach them better and lovingly touched the top of his head.

"Stop teasing me! I have finally sat down after seeing to the household. Now what mischief are you up to today?" she asked, gently putting down her teacup.

"Mischief? Me? What makes you ask that, Ma?" he asked innocently. Settling himself on the floor at his mother's side, he reached out and helped himself to a piece of shondesh, a traditional Bengali sweet, from a tray in front of his mother.

His mother slapped his hand indulgently, but then moved the plate to within his reach.

Eyeing him with mock criticism, she switched to her faultless English and said, "Well, first of all you are dressed in your best day clothes, although I still do not like that waistcoat. You should really buy yourself some new clothes, my son."

Julian's smile faded. "Ma, these clothes are perfectly

serviceable. You know that what I wear doesn't make a whit of difference to how they treat me. . . ."

Then his smile returned. "But that doesn't mean I can't dress well—and the waistcoat does show off my eyes, doesn't it?"

"Yes, it does," his mother replied indulgently. "You look very handsome. So, tell me, where have you been visiting looking so nice?"

"Oh, just to the home of Sir Lionel," Julian said as nonchalantly as he could. "Is there any lemonade? It is getting quite warm out."

"Do not try and puff me off, Julian. I know you have been up to something!" his mother said.

"I am not trying to puff you off. I did go to Sir Lionel's house," he insisted, and then added with a grin, "And it is very warm out."

He should have known that he would not be able to put one over on his mother—she was too sharp. He laughed quietly to himself when he thought of all the times he had tried to hide something from her. She had always found out.

She rose and, slightly adjusting her flowing sari, moved to the door to ask a servant to fetch lemonade for her son. Returning, she said with a little smile, "Perhaps I should ask not where you have been, but whom you have met?"

"Miss Renwick. And Lady Renwick, of course," he answered honestly, but did not volunteer any more information than that.

His mother's curved eyebrows rose, but the smile faded from her face. "Ah, *Miss* Renwick! Tell me more about this Miss Renwick."

"She just arrived from England two weeks ago. I met her last night at the ball I attended," Julian explained.

"I suppose that explains the nice clothes."

He laughed and then took a drink from the lemonade handed to him by a servant. "Yes, well, I did want to make a good impression."

He paused as he put down his drink. "Lady Renwick, however, dismissed me almost the minute she saw me."

His mother's face sobered. "That woman!"

"Now, now, Ma. You know how she is. She has never been kind to me. She simply will not accept me, because . . ." Julian left his sentence unfinished. They both knew exactly why Lady Renwick would not accept Julian.

His mother's face lost all good humor. She looked down at her hands. "It is not as if you were completely abandoned by your father, like so many," she said quietly. "If only he had not returned to England. But I expect another letter from him any day now," she added hopefully.

A period of silence followed. The anger that Julian had felt the previous night after learning of Reggie's promotion simmered in his stomach once again, only this time it burned even hotter.

Julian sipped his lemonade but said nothing. There was, after all, nothing to say that had not already been said before, and it only upset her when he became angry.

He tried to cool his temper. "Miss Renwick is a very beautiful young lady," he said.

His mother's eyes snapped up to his. "Julian! You should not get any ideas," she said vehemently.

He knew that she did not want him to get hurt any more by these bigoted English, but it was too late. His entire life had been spent fighting to be accepted by the English, as one of them.

It would never happen. His mother had tried to tell him so numerous times. She was as sure of this as she was that her own heritage was impeccable.

But it was her heritage that caused him to be an outcast. It was not good enough that her family had been wealthy landowners for countless generations. The English saw only the color of their skin and thought less of them because they were dark.

Julian put down his lemonade and got up to pace the

length of the long room. It was a meager attempt to control his emotions and it did not work.

"Why should I not meet with Miss Renwick? She is a very pretty and eligible young lady." He could not accept his fate. He could not and he would not.

He bumped into the delicate inlaid wooden table on the other side of the room. He did not know why his mother insisted on having all this European-style furniture in her drawing room, since they almost never entertained.

The sofas, chairs and tables, all of the finest workmanship, had sat here unused nearly all of his life—remnants from his father's influence and of his mother's hope that someday her husband would return to her. Julian restrained the urge to do physical damage to his mother's English furniture.

"Julian, you know very well why not," his mother was saying. She had risen too.

Putting a gentle, calming hand on his arm, she looked up at him, her soft brown eyes filled with sadness. "Do not do this, Julian. Please, do not. . . ."

Julian took a step away from her. He could not look her in the eye. Once again she had discerned his intention without his having to say a word. Her ability to read him was uncanny.

"I am sorry, Mother, but it is something I have to do," he said.

Before he left the room, Julian sketched a very English little bow.

The events of the previous evening were the main topic in Mrs. Hurst's drawing room later that morning, with Lady Renwick dominating the conversation.

Cassandra sat quietly in an overstuffed chair, feeling small and insignificant. This was not unusual for Cassandra. She had often felt that way when making morning calls in London—especially during her last two weeks there while waiting for the ship that would take her to Calcutta.

She pushed herself to the edge of the chair and held her back straight. So many years of sitting on hard wooden benches at Miss Stillwater's with her back perfectly straight now allowed her to maintain her dignity with relative ease. She was grateful that morning calls in Calcutta were more easily dealt with and suffered through than they had been in London.

As far as she knew, no one here was aware of her relationship with Lord Felbridge. And she could only hope that no one learned of it—she had no desire to become the laughingstock of Calcutta society as well.

"It is not at all surprising that Cassandra should be the talk of town. She is certainly the prettiest girl in Calcutta, if I may say so myself," Lady Renwick said, after fortifying herself with a sip of her tea.

The comment made Cassandra flinch and pay more attention to the conversation at hand.

"Oh, but Lady Renwick, you are so right! You are lucky to be blessed with such a lovely daughter, as am I," Mrs. Hurst said, passing her a plate of lemon tarts.

Cassandra looked down at the teacup carefully balanced in her hands. She wondered if Miss Hurst felt as embarrassed by this conversation as she did.

A glance in her direction immediately put that quandary to rest. The young woman in question seemed to take her mother's compliment as if it was nothing but an obvious statement of fact.

Cassandra supposed that it was, since the girl was indeed very pretty. She was fashionably dark, with rich brown curls, hazel eyes and an excellent figure. And there was certainly no question that she knew just how beautiful she was.

"Oh, but Miss Hurst is much prettier than I," Cassandra said, trying to be polite by joining in the conversation. "And there seemed to be very few girls at the ball last night who were not engaged for nearly every dance."

"But there are so few young ladies compared to the number of gentlemen. It would be surprising if they didn't all dance. Why, even Miss Prattlesworth danced every dance—and she has squinty eyes and never stops talking!" Miss Hurst said, smoothing back her perfectly coifed hair.

"Indeed, my dear, the shortage of young ladies does make things so difficult," Mrs. Hurst agreed. "Why, I noticed that even you, Miss Renwick, were obliged to dance with that awful Mr. Ritchie. However did you manage to get caught by him?"

Cassandra looked at her hostess with a burning desire to give her a scathing response. Instead, she took a deep breath and then plastered a smile on her face.

"I was not 'caught by him,' Mrs. Hurst. I was honored that he asked me to dance. He is an excellent dancer and a very pleasant gentleman."

Cassandra could feel her mother's eyes boring into her. She was sure that she would pay for her comments later. But for now, it did feel good to speak up for the poor man who was so wronged only because he did not hold a very high position. It was terrible to treat people with such cruelty, as she very well knew from personal experience!

Mrs. Hurst gave a very offended sniff. "Well, I only hope for your sake that you did not completely destroy your reputation with that bit of high jinks. You should count yourself extremely lucky that your mother is so very well-respected."

Cassandra bit her tongue to keep herself from making a sharp retort. She didn't want to get into any more trouble than she was in already.

Satisfied that she had won the exchange, Mrs. Hurst gave Cassandra a smug little smile. But her mother could not leave it there.

"Poor Cassandra does not yet know the ways of Calcutta society, Adelaide. I am sure that her little faux pas will be quickly overlooked."

Mrs. Hurst's smile began to look as if it were hurting her to keep it where it was, but she persevered. "Of course, you are right, Caroline."

She then turned to her daughter, who did not even try to hide the look of smug contempt on her face. "Before you arrived, Miss Renwick, my dear Anne was considered the reigning incomparable of the season. Now, I suppose she shall have to share that title with you, won't you, my dear?"

Miss Hurst lost her smug look very quickly. A pointed look from her mother, and she pasted a smile on to her face.

"Yes," she said, as if the word had been pulled from her throat.

"Well, I certainly have no desire to take away your position, Miss Hurst . . ."

"My dear, you are not taking it away, you are simply going to share it. And besides, it is entirely fitting that you should do so—why, with your mother's position and your natural charm and beauty, it is well deserved," Lady Hurst said, giving Lady Renwick a toad-eating smile.

"And I am sure that, as your dear mother said, you shall learn how to go on soon enough. At least, let us hope that you do."

After a full morning of visiting, when they had had to also stop at the drawing rooms of Mrs. Trotter, Mrs. Parkinson, as well as Lady Georgina Wright, Lady Renwick was ready for a nap. Cassandra, however, was restless. She had had her fill of social calls when she had been in London and had truly hoped to get away from the pressures of society in Calcutta. Still, she recognized that nothing she could do could convince her mother that she just wished to live quietly for some time.

Walking into the cool darkness toward the back of the house, Cassandra thought she would try and take her mind off of society. Her father's library had a wonderful collection of books. Perhaps she could find something that would increase her understanding of this strange land.

She had certainly enjoyed perusing the shelves the other night as her father had sat working at his large mahogany desk. Hopefully, she would find something stimulating again today.

As she pushed open the closed door, her eyes were dazzled by the bright sunlight that flooded in through the large windows.

"Excuse me, Miss Renwick, is there something I can help you find?"

Her breath caught in her throat as her eyes adjusted to the light and she saw Mr. Ritchie standing at her father's desk with some papers in his hand. A warmth rushed through her at the sight of him. She was sure she must be blushing.

"Oh, I am sorry, Mr. Ritchie, I did not know you were here!"

She put a hand to her cheek. "I have just returned from paying morning visits with my mother. It . . . it has become very warm out," she stammered by way of explanation for her bright red cheeks.

"Indeed, it becomes quite hot at this time of day." He smiled at her, warming her even further.

"I just came in to find a book," Cassandra said, moving to the bookshelves closest to the door.

"Ah, then I won't disturb you."

"Oh no, I am sure it is I who am disturbing you from your work."

Mr. Ritchie shifted the papers in his hands, a smile tugging at the corner of his mouth. "But it is a pleasant disturbance, so please take your time."

Cassandra giggled. He was so sweet—a little shy or perhaps awkward, but with a presence that made him very attractive.

She attempted to search through the books, but did not actually read one title—she was too distracted. It seemed as if Mr. Ritchie, too, was having difficulty focusing on his work.

Finally, he said, "At about five o'clock the weather cools down quite nicely. I . . . I would be honored if you would go riding with me at that time. Just . . . for a bit of exercise."

"Oh, that sounds wonderful. I would love to!" Cassandra could not stop the enthusiasm from entering her voice.

Mr. Ritchie smiled, but his expression became a little clouded as he remembered propriety. "I . . . I believe you should ask your mother first."

"Yes, I will do so," she said, but already she knew what the answer would be.

Perhaps it was for the best, Cassandra sighed, as she softly closed the door to the office behind her. She did not want to become interested in a man only to have her heart broken again. No, it would be better to stay away from Mr. Ritchie.

Although, she thought, slowly walking down the hallway turning over the book she had picked at random, perhaps it wouldn't hurt to ask her mother if she could go riding with him.

After all, what harm could one little ride do?

4

As expected, her mother did not agree.

"But Mama, why ever not? What have you got against Mr. Ritchie? Is it just because he works for Papa?" Cassandra asked, tucking her feet up under her in the soft overstuffed chair of the informal drawing room where she and her mother were sitting.

Lady Renwick sighed and put down the embroidery on which she had been working. "You may have learned proper deportment and the social graces of a young lady at that school I sent you to, but I am certain they never touched on the particularities of Calcutta society. It is high time you learned about it, however, since somehow I did not do a good job of explaining things to you this morning.

"Cassandra, Mr. Ritchie is not one of us. It is not just that he is a clerk, which is certainly no point in his favor. Even if he were an Englishman, I would never allow you to go riding with a mere clerk. But my point is that he is not a full-blooded Englishman."

Lady Renwick paused for effect and then exclaimed dramatically, "He is a half-breed!"

Cassandra looked even more confused. "A half-breed? What is that?"

"A half-breed is a Eurasian, my dear. His father is

English and his mother Indian. He has no place in our society."

Lady Renwick picked up her embroidery again. "I am sure you understand and will spurn any advances he makes. They are totally inappropriate from one in his position." She paused and then said partially under her breath, "Although Mr. Ritchie has remained particularly obtuse, I expect that someday he will learn his proper place."

Cassandra closed her mouth with a snap. It must have fallen open with her mother's explanation, although she hadn't been aware of it.

Suddenly everything made sense.

This was why people had turned their backs on Mr. Ritchie at the ball. This was why Major Vernon had frowned at her so fiercely when she had shown an interest in him.

And it also explained his unusual coloring. His features, including his brilliant eyes, must be inherited from his father, and his hair and skin color from his mother. What a striking combination!

But it still wasn't right. No matter what his birth, no one should be treated the way Mr. Ritchie had been.

Lady Renwick gave a nod of approval at her daughter's silence. "Now that you understand how things work, Cassandra, I trust that you will no longer give a thought to your father's clerk. I do believe, however, that Major Vernon is going to be present at Lady Minto's soiree tomorrow evening. We shall attend, of course. Everyone will be there."

Cassandra did not even acknowledge her mother's chatter about who would attend the soiree. She just could not imagine how her mother could expect her to just forget about Mr. Ritchie.

Cassandra began to tap her fingers together, her hands steepled in her lap.

How could she just sit back and allow someone to be treated so cruelly? Had she not just suffered the same injustice at the hands of Lord Felbridge? How could her mother not see the similarity?

She locked her fingers together. She could feel all of her muscles tense in her growing anger.

Finally, she could not stand it any longer. "Mama," Cassandra tried to interrupt her mother's prattle.

". . . and when they danced, why, you could just see that he was all wrong. . . ."

"Mother!" Cassandra worked to keep herself from shouting.

"What is it?" Her mother looked up in surprise from her embroidery.

"Mama, don't you see that what you are doing is wrong?"

"Wrong?" She held her embroidery out to examine the flower she had been stitching. "I admit the colors are not exactly right. . . ."

"No! Not your sewing! Mr. Ritchie."

"What, are you still thinking about him? I thought we had resolved that."

"No, Mama, we have not. Don't you see that the way you treat Mr. Ritchie is exactly the same way that I was treated in London? You are discriminating against him because of who his parents are. Can you not see that is wrong?"

Lady Renwick looked at her daughter as if she had lost her mind. "Your parents, Cassandra, are both English. If you were discriminated against because of that, it is the first I have ever heard of such a thing."

"No, Mama, I was laughed at because I had thought to marry a viscount when my father is only a baronet. It is the same thing. You look down on Mr. Ritchie because his mother is Indian."

Her mother looked blankly at her. "I do not see the similarity."

Cassandra sighed. "It is not Mr. Ritchie's fault that his mother is Indian, just like it is not my fault that Papa is a baronet. He should not be discriminated against because of who his mother is," she explained as patiently as she could.

Cassandra paused. "In fact, I believe, it is what makes him so interesting. He bridges two cultures."

Her mother scowled and turned back to her embroidery. "Cassandra, you are too young to understand. You must simply accept what I say and stay away from Mr. Ritchie."

Lady Renwick shuddered dramatically. "Bridging two cultures indeed. As if anyone would have the slightest interest in Indian culture, if you can call it that. Why they are nothing more than dirty heathens!"

With a groan of frustration, Cassandra got up and ran to her bedroom.

In her room, she paced back and forth. How could her mother not understand? How could she treat people this way? Oh, she wanted to scream!

No. She had to calm down. She took a deep breath. There had to be some way to get through to her mother and to others in English society. How could these people live in a foreign country and have no interest in it or its people? She just did not understand.

Of course, she thought as she dropped down into the chair in front of her dressing table, if she could learn more about Indian culture and, even possibly, what it was like to be a Eurasian, then maybe she could help change the way people thought. Was it possible? Could *she* make a difference?

She didn't know, but it was certainly worth a try. And she had to do something.

Julian left through a side door just as Miss Renwick was coming out the front gates.

"It is a pleasant time for a walk, is it not, Miss Renwick?" he said, moving quickly forward so that he could walk alongside her.

"Oh, Mr. Ritchie, what a pleasant surprise! Are you on your way home?"

"Not quite yet. I still have some more work to do. I just thought I might step out for a bit of fresh air."

Miss Renwick gave a little nod of her head. Although she kept her eyes looking forward, she did not hide the look of pleasure that crossed her face.

"Calcutta is a fascinating city. There are such opposites existing side by side. I am just amazed at the incredible differences between the palatial homes of the British and the Indian nobility and the huts of the poor natives."

Julian looked at her, surprised at her perceptive mind. He had never known anyone to openly comment on the vast differences between the poor Indians and the English, and to find it interesting was quite beyond what he would have expected from such a pretty English girl.

He looked back at the Renwicks' house, seeing it through her eyes. It was no exception to the standard design of British homes—quite large with numerous bedrooms and drawing rooms. There were also two other buildings within the compound—one was the servants' quarters, the other the kitchen.

But just outside the gates were small cottages with thatched roofs. Even Julian did not know who lived there, despite the fact that he had passed these houses nearly every day for the past two years.

They walked past the cottages slowly, trying not to stare. Miss Renwick scrunched up her nose at all the smells that assailed them. They were so familiar to Julian that he almost did not notice them, but seeing Miss Renwick's reaction brought the smells to his attention.

It was a heady combination of flowers, some delicious spicy cooking odors—frying chili peppers which burned the throat and sent them coughing—and the smell from the cows, chickens, and goats that wandered about freely.

Miss Renwick smiled at the wide-eyed stares of two women cooking their dinner over an open flame just in front of their door. The women had been gossiping, but stopped abruptly at their approach. They stared at Miss Renwick in particular, as did the children who had ceased their playing to watch the white lady walk by.

In the sudden silence of the street, a loud shout and a child's cry caught their attention.

Slightly farther down the road was one of the commonly seen roadside tea stands. The noise was centered around a young boy, who was squatting on the ground next to an overturned pot of steaming tea and some broken clay cups.

It was clear that the boy had been trying to carefully pour the hot tea into the cups when the pot had slipped out of his grasp. From the way he was holding his hand, it looked as if he might have burned himself.

Miss Renwick gasped as the man standing over the boy suddenly bent over and slapped him so hard that the child was knocked to the ground.

Letting out an outraged exclamation, she drew up her skirts and ran full-tilt to the tea stand.

"How could you hit a child that way?" she cried out at the man. Then, completely heedless of her dress, or the very interested audience that was quickly gathering to watch, she gently picked up the boy in her arms.

The man who had been yelling at the boy stopped speaking in mid-sentence. Rendered abruptly speechless, he stood with his mouth hanging open, staring at the young Englishwoman.

Julian had also been momentarily frozen by Miss Renwick's shocking behavior. But he now quickly moved to her side. "Miss Renwick, please put him down. This is none of our business. We should not get involved."

Miss Renwick turned to him, her pale blue eyes filled with tears of distress. "How could I put the poor thing down? I cannot stand by and watch a child be abused."

"But truly, this is none of our concern. Please, put the child down," Julian implored. He could see the tea merchant beginning to get angry and knew he had every right to be. Why she felt the need to interfere was beyond both his and the merchant's comprehension.

"Oh please, Miss, he is filthy!" Miss Renwick's maid, who had been walking behind them, joined in the fray.

"Nonsense! As if I would let a little dirt bother me. Come, Gita, we will take him home, and see to him."

"Oh no, Miss! You should not even think of doing so!"

"No, honestly, Miss Renwick . . ." Julian began.

Miss Renwick ignored them both and turned to the man. "Are you the boy's father?"

The man looked curiously at Julian and the maid, clearly not understanding any English. Gita translated her mistress's question into Bengali.

The man shook his head. "Baba nei, Ma o nei."

Understanding that the child was an orphan, Miss Renwick nodded with authority. "Then we shall relieve you of your responsibility to the child."

She then turned and marched back the way she had come, the boy still held in her arms. Julian ran after her, leaving Gita to translate as best as she could.

He contemplated arguing with her during the short walk back to the Renwicks' home, but the determined set of her chin stopped him. He had seen such abuse so many times in his life and yet he had never thought to intervene. But this young woman, new to Calcutta, had done what no one else would have had the courage to do.

Julian could not stop his admiration for her from growing as the significance of her actions solidified in his mind.

They ignored the man's impotent shouts that his property had just been stolen from him. Both he and Gita knew well that no one was going to challenge the young memsahib for a street urchin.

Gita kept silent through the walk back to the house. But she was moved to protest once more when Miss Renwick paused to walk up the few steps to the front door of her parents' house.

"Oh no, Miss, what would your mother say?"

At that Miss Renwick finally stopped, turned around and came back down the couple of steps she had taken.

"But where else shall I take him?" she asked quietly, with a stricken expression on her face. Julian could see that the enormity of what she had done had begun to dawn on her.

"Come to the servants' quarters," he directed gently.

Miss Renwick nodded and followed him around the house to the back. Gita led them into a large room where straw mats were laid out along one wall.

"This is where the menservants sleep," she said.

Miss Renwick nodded and laid the boy down on one of the mats. Julian, standing behind her, looked down to find terror-filled liquid brown eyes staring up at them.

Smoothing the boy's hair, Miss Renwick said reassuringly, "It is all right. I will care for you now."

Gita translated, but they were all surprised when he looked directly at Miss Renwick and clearly said, "Memsahib, rice eat?" and motioned with his hand to his mouth.

Miss Renwick smiled broadly at him and then up at Julian. "He does know some English. I am certain that he will quickly learn more."

She nodded to Gita. "Get the poor thing some food and then we will give him a bath. And could you please try to find some clean clothes for him as well?"

Gita looked at Julian for guidance, but he nodded his assent. They would probably all get into trouble for this, but there was nothing to be done about it now.

After she had gone, Miss Renwick turned back to the boy. "What is your name?" she asked slowly.

"Harishchandra Paramanik," he answered, puffing up his skinny chest.

Julian nearly laughed at the pride in the boy's voice. Miss Renwick just blinked at him and then smiled slowly. "May I just call you Harry? Is that all right?"

The boy seemed to understand and smiled up at them. But his attention turned quickly to Gita, who had returned with a large bowl of food.

"Sir Lionel is looking for you, sahib," she said to Julian.

He had nearly forgotten that he was supposed to be working. Although reluctant to leave the touching scene that was unfolding here, he knew that the maid would see to both the boy and her mistress.

Cassandra acknowledged Mr. Ritchie's quick good-byes, but her attention was entirely on Harry. The urchin was sitting up, and, with eyes as wide as saucers, was gesturing to the plate in Gita's hand. He said something to her in Bengali, looking at her quizzically.

Gita looked down at the one plate, then began blinking back the tears in her eyes. "He wants to know if we will be sharing the food with him," she said softly, translating the boy's question.

Cassandra was confused. "Is that the custom?" she asked.

Gita shook her head. "The child has never been given so much food before. To us it is a normal, even a small helping, but to him it is an incredible amount of food."

With a catch in her voice, Cassandra told her to tell the boy that it was all for him and there would be more if he wanted it.

But first he had to bathe.

Clearly Harry did not like the idea of a bath at all. But the thought of having all that food, and more, helped to persuade him that it would be worth it.

Gita led Harry and Cassandra out to the side of the house, where a bucket of water had been drawn for him. To the sound of loud and fervent protests from Harry, he was quickly and efficiently scrubbed from head to toe. It was a sweet smelling boy, albeit dressed in clothes that were much too large for him, who finally went back to his room to eat his meal.

Exhaustion overtook young Harry immediately after eating. With a full belly after all of the excitement of the afternoon, Harry's long-lashed eyes closed and his anxious face relaxed as he gently fell asleep.

The following evening, Cassandra dressed with care for the Governor-General's soiree. She wanted to look particularly fine in the hopes that she might have a word with the Governor-General about the treatment of people of mixed race.

She had never been one to fight for the cause of another or get involved in politics, but she supposed that it was never too late to start. As in the case with little Harry, she suddenly found herself wanting to do more for others than she had ever even considered.

Gita carefully wove small white flowers through Cassandra's golden ringlets. As she watched in the mirror, Cassandra could not help but remember the beautiful fragrant white flowers Mr. Ritchie had wound around her hair the day before.

These were not the same—in more ways than one.

After Gita finished her hair, Cassandra took out her writing materials. After only a moment's hesitation, she wrote a note to Mr. Ritchie, requesting him to accompany her for a ride the following morning at seven.

She had learned that it was common practice to go riding early in the morning before the day became too hot. And, Cassandra thought, her mother would not be awake that early to object.

If she truly wanted to do something to help Mr. Ritchie and others like him, then she figured the best person to go to for information would be Mr. Ritchie himself.

She bit her lip as she turned to hand the note to a waiting servant. To her surprise, it was little Harry who stood waiting to deliver her note.

He had somehow managed to fashion for himself a smaller version of the household livery, complete with a white turban and a peacock feather gently waving atop his head.

Trying hard to keep the smile from her lips, she handed the note to the very determined-looking boy. It seemed as if he was going to take his new duties quite seriously.

"Please deliver this note to Mr. Ritchie, Harry. Make sure he gets it in his own hands." Cassandra transferred the note from one hand to the other to show the boy what she meant, in case he did not fully understand her English.

Harry repeated, "Note Mr. Ritchie, I give."

Cassandra smiled, thrilled that he had understood her. "Yes, you give him the note."

Harry salaamed, backed away, then turned and ran off with the note. It was only after he left that Cassandra realized that neither she nor Harry knew where Mr. Ritchie lived.

5

The Governor-General's house in Calcutta was a classic Georgian edifice, although its opulence reminded Cassandra of a palace. It seemed rather isolated in a large park that had just been planted with young trees, although the flower gardens were meticulously cared for.

As Cassandra stepped down from the carriage, she was nearly overwhelmed by the heady fragrance emanating from enormous bouquets of aromatic Indian flowers amassed on either side of the doorway.

As her mother had predicted, the soirce was indeed attended by all of the most fashionable people in Calcutta. The open rooms were crowded with people, reminding Cassandra of the few London parties she had attended.

Just minutes after entering the room, Lady Renwick curtly whispered in her ear, needlessly pointing out the significance of Major Vernon's presence at her side.

Cassandra was determined not to have to endure yet another scolding from her mother. She made sure she was on her very best behavior. Giving Major Vernon her prettiest, most welcoming smile, she allowed him to lead her on to the dance floor, where a country dance was just forming.

As it ended, he escorted Cassandra back to her mother, who was sitting on a small sofa conversing with Lord and

Lady Minto. Lady Renwick proudly reintroduced her daughter to the Governor-General and his wife.

Lady Minto acknowledged Cassandra before continuing her discussion with Lady Renwick about the lack of good household help in India. Meanwhile, as Lord Minto gallantly relinquished his seat to Cassandra, the ever-ambitious Major Vernon took the opportunity to engage him in conversation.

Cassandra half-listened to the two conversations around her as she surreptitiously scanned the assemblage for a dark head that was figuring in her thoughts with disturbing frequency. Although she had understood from her mother that Mr. Ritchie would not be invited to the Governor-General's residence, she realized that his absence still caused her more than a twinge of disappointment.

Her attention was caught, however, by the slightly raised voice of Major Vernon as he argued with Lord Minto.

"Well, frankly, my lord, no! I disagree with your proposal. We should *not* encourage more natives to be educated. It is unnecessary, and, quite frankly, I do not believe they are capable of it."

Cassandra could not help but laugh aloud at the absurdity of his statement. She interrupted the men. "Do you mean, my lord, that the Indians are not allowed to be educated?"

Lord Minto turned to her, with an amused and curious expression on his face. "It is not that they are not allowed, Miss Renwick, it is just that we do not have the facilities to educate them in the best of English tradition. The wealthiest, of course, are well educated—there is the one Indian school. But I am proposing to allow more Indian boys into Hindu College, where the English boys now attend classes."

"That would be wonderful, sir. Are you proposing this for all Indians, or only the ones of mixed blood?"

"Oh, no, Miss Renwick, for all natives. Many, if not most of the Eurasians, are already educated with our boys."

Major Vernon smiled indulgently at Cassandra. "My dear Miss Renwick, I am so sorry! This must be terribly boring for you. You surely cannot be interested in such dull stuff as the education of the natives."

"Oh, but I am, Major Vernon. It is quite interesting to me. Here I am in India, and I know almost nothing about the country, or its people. Is it not absurd?"

She smiled at him, inviting him to share in her amusement.

Major Vernon clearly found nothing amusing, and his face took on a serious mien. "No, I would not say it is absurd. You are a good English girl and really should not concern yourself with such things."

"Why ever not?" asked Cassandra, beginning to get irritated with Major Vernon's condescending attitude.

Lord Minto laughed at the two young people. "I believe, Miss Renwick, that Major Vernon feels that good English girls should only concern themselves with pretty dresses and finding a proper husband."

"Yes, that is it, exactly," agreed Major Vernon, oblivious to Cassandra's growing anger.

"Do you not believe that I should take an interest in the world around me? Or do you think that I am too foolish, as you clearly believe the Indians to be?" Cassandra was very close to losing her temper. She had an extreme dislike of being spoken down to.

Lady Renwick, although deep in conversation with Lady Minto, had heard Cassandra's angry tone of voice, and quickly jumped in before her daughter completely disgraced herself.

"Cassandra, my dear, I do believe that you should leave the more serious discussions to the men. Gentlemen, you will, of course, excuse my daughter. She has recently come from school and is not quite used to interacting in a social setting."

Lady Renwick managed to smile charmingly at the two gentlemen while making it clear to Cassandra that she was out of line.

After her mother's quelling look, Cassandra realized that she would do better to stay quiet for some time. She sat with her mouth clamped shut, trying to calm her quickly beating heart.

After all, the Governor-General seemed to be an eminently sensible man. She decided to put her faith in him—at least so far as educating Indians was concerned.

Julian stepped out of the door of his home and was immediately brought up short by a young boy in familiar livery. For a moment he did not recognize the street urchin Miss Renwick had saved the previous day. This boy walked proudly and spoke with assurance.

"Mr. Ritchie?" the boy asked in a strong Bengali accent.

"Yes?" Julian replied, managing to keep a serious expression on his face.

The boy handed him a folded piece of paper, salaamed and then turned and walked off officiously.

Julian had to keep himself from laughing out loud at the child's self-importance. But then he turned his attention to the note in his hand.

As he quickly scanned the lines, a low whistle escaped his lips. He tucked the paper into his coat's tail pocket and continued on his way to Reggie's home for their dinner engagement.

Reggie shared an Indian cook, originally from the nearby French colony of Chandernagore, with the man who lived in the flat below his. This excellent chef was one reason why Julian frequently invited himself to partake of his friend's hospitality.

After a superb French meal, the two men retired to Reggie's drawing room. There they sat in contented, companionable silence, nursing their brandies, each deep in his own thoughts.

After a while, Julian looked over at his friend, who seemed to be analyzing the amber liquid in his glass. Making a decision, he pulled out the note from his pocket.

After perusing it once more, he said, "Reggie, you are a very good friend."

"Well," Reggie blurted at this bald statement, "I should hope so!"

"Yes. Well, you remember the plan I told you I was working on the other night when I was here?"

Reggie immediately sat up, his body tense and ready. "I remember it only too well."

"Tonight I received this." He held up the note young Harry had handed him. "It is the sign that I was waiting for."

"What do you mean, the sign? What is it?"

"I am going to share this with you, Reggie, *because* you are such a good friend and I know that it will go no farther than these walls." Julian hesitated and then handed him the note.

Reggie scanned the note with curiosity. "By Jove!" he exclaimed, clucking disapprovingly with his tongue.

Julian leaned back in his chair. "Well? What do you think?"

Reggie's eyes grew large. "But is it not obvious, my boy? You must send her a note back explaining that it is impossible to meet her in such a way."

"Must I?" Julian said, quirking one eyebrow at his friend.

"But, of course!" Reggie got up and paced about the room, clearly agitated by his friend's cool acceptance of this scandalous assignation.

Julian nodded his head and pursed his lips together in thought. "Perhaps I should. But you know that I will not. Not after all that I have been through at the hands of Lady Renwick. I could not possibly pass up an opportunity like this."

As Julian emptied his glass and moved to fill it once more, Reggie continued his agitated entreaties. "Julian, really, this girl does not know what she is doing. She cannot know the significance of asking you to go riding without her mother's approval."

"Perhaps she does not," Julian said, "but I do."

Reggie stopped his pacing directly in front of Julian. His mouth opened and closed a few times before he was finally able to express himself. "Julian, this chit is a complete innocent. You cannot simply meet her like this!"

Julian looked up at his friend, but said nothing, so Reggie went on, "Not only that, she is the daughter of our employer. Have you given any thought to that?"

Reggie resumed his pacing. "Have you really mulled over the implications? What do you think Sir Lionel would do if he found out that his daughter had even sent you such a note? By God, you would be cast out without a reference, without . . . without . . ." Reggie sputtered, horrified at the thought.

"Without a penny," Julian finished for him. "I don't believe he would, by the way. I don't believe he has the backbone to do that. But Reggie, he is not going to find out, is he?" Julian leaned forward meaningfully.

"He had better well not, I should say."

"And so should I." Julian looked closely at his friend, who had stopped his frenetic pacing.

Reggie caught Julian's eye. "Do you think that I would tell him? Devil a bit, what kind of friend do you think I am, Julian?"

"A very good one, as I have already said. Otherwise, I would never have shown the note to you." Julian sat back, at his ease.

Reggie relaxed a bit as well and sat down again on the settee across from Julian. "Honestly, Julian, you aren't actually going to meet her?"

Julian sighed. "Yes, Reggie, I am. I am going to meet her tomorrow and possibly the next day and the next. I am going to meet her as often as I can."

Then, with a rueful smile playing on his face, he continued, "And I tell you now, Reggie, that sweet, innocent, beautiful girl is going to fall head over heels in love with me. And her mother is going to pay for all of the years of torment she has made me suffer. Oh yes, she is going to pay!"

6

"Good morning, Mr. Ritchie. I hope you are well today?" Cassandra said, trying to sound as if meeting a gentleman for an early morning ride was an ordinary occurrence.

"Very well, Miss Renwick, thank you," Mr. Ritchie said, playing along.

Cassandra released the breath she hadn't realized she was holding.

This was going to be all right. He was going to be a gentleman and not mention her bold invitation or how inappropriate it was for her to even suggest that they meet like this.

She hadn't been sure how he would react to her invitation, but his easy manner, as if this were a normal occurrence, dispelled some of her tension.

She still wasn't entirely sure that she would have the courage to do what she planned.

Mr. Ritchie turned his horse, leading her away from Chowringhee Road, where other riders were out taking their exercise.

Cassandra could not help but notice that Mr. Ritchie was an excellent horseman. The strong, yet easy gait of his horse showed his muscular thighs and powerful hands to advantage.

Not that she was interested in such things—but, simply from an aesthetic point of view, it was a pleasing sight.

Cassandra swallowed hard and tried to remember all the things she had planned to ask him. However, somehow, now that she was in his presence, she couldn't think of one thing other than his very male presence.

She looked away and tried again to focus her mind. Last evening while lying in bed, she had decided that she wanted to question Mr. Ritchie while they were riding. She wanted to learn more about his life here in Calcutta, and how he dealt with the treatment he received from the English here with such equanimity.

But now that she was with him, the thought of asking such questions turned Cassandra's bones to jelly. She hated to admit this to herself, but she was a coward. She just could not ask this man such personal questions.

"I thought I might show you some of Calcutta, if you are interested," Mr. Ritchie said, as they rode across a large open field.

Cassandra had been so involved in her own thoughts that she hadn't even noticed where they were going. Now, however, she looked around her.

They were riding across a large expanse of grass where herds of goats and cows grazed. The scene rather reminded Cassandra of Hyde Park, but with fewer trees and many more animals.

Keeping the animals together were boys wielding long sticks. Their skins were dark brown from days spent out in the sun, but their eyes were bright and alert for anything unusual—like a white woman out riding with a brown-skinned man.

Cassandra ignored their stares and saw that it was going to be a bright, beautiful day. The sun, just newly risen, had not yet dispelled the cool of the night, so the temperature was still very comfortable.

She looked over at Mr. Ritchie who gave her a sweet smile, his white teeth standing out from his bronze face.

Just seeing him smile at her made Cassandra lose more of her tension.

It was rather a shame that she was not interested in men, for if she was, Mr. Ritchie would certainly be someone who she could find very attractive. She nearly shook her head at her silliness. She was not interested in men.

As the park ended, they entered the streets of the city itself. Mr. Ritchie pointed out buildings of interest to Cassandra as they rode along—the Writers' Building, where her father's office was, St. John's Cathedral, the Supreme Court, and the homes of many influential people.

The scene around looked like it could have been anywhere in the central part of London. Only the coolies with their baskets on their heads, and the Indian women in their brilliantly colored saris, reminded Cassandra that she was indeed in India. Cassandra was fascinated by everything she saw.

"I now understand why Calcutta is called the City of Palaces. These magnificent buildings and wide boulevards are quite awe-inspiring," she commented.

"I must admit, I am quite proud of my city. And I am honored to have been given this opportunity to show it off to you."

Cassandra felt her cheeks warm as she blushed. "I . . . I thank you, sir." She gave herself a mental shake and reminded herself once more why she had asked for this ride.

"You certainly know Calcutta very well," she said, trying to guide their conversation to a place where she could ask him some of her questions.

"Well, yes, of course. I have lived here all my life," Mr. Ritchie said, smiling warmly at her.

Cassandra swallowed. "I was speaking with the Governor-General last night at the soiree I attended. He mentioned that he wanted to enlarge Hindu College so that more natives could attend."

"Lord Minto is a very thoughtful man and he has good intentions," Mr. Ritchie said, losing his easy smile.

"But?"

He looked at her. A sadness had somehow crept into his eyes that had not been there earlier. "But, I do not believe that it will happen."

Before Cassandra could probe him further, Mr. Ritchie spurred his horse forward. "Calcutta has many small winding streets, such as this." He pointed down the street to their left. "You must be careful where you ride, Miss Renwick, or else it is very easy to get lost."

Cassandra reined in her horse at the corner. "Do you ever get lost, Mr. Ritchie?" she asked, playing along with him.

His quick smile returned to his face. "Not often. I told you, I have lived here my entire life."

"Then tell me where this street leads," she teased.

He laughed. "It leads to Chandney Chawk Bazaar, where the less wealthy Europeans live, as well as many natives."

"Do all Indians live very differently from us?" Cassandra asked, deliberately including Julian among the English.

Mr. Ritchie took a moment to answer, looking into Cassandra's eyes so deeply a slight shiver ran down her arms. "Yes, we do, very differently," he finally said.

"We, Mr. Ritchie?" Cassandra took a deep breath and finally asked what had been going through her mind ever since she had found out about his heritage. "Do you consider yourself more Indian or English?"

He was clearly caught off-guard by her forthright question. His face lost its good humor, but then he regained his equilibrium and said, "I am equally comfortable in both worlds, Miss Renwick, but accepted in neither."

He turned his horse away and led her back the way they had come. The ride back was silent and strained. For Cassandra, the magic and wonder of the morning had vanished. Her throat tightened with suppressed emotion.

How could she have done that? She had completely ruined their ride. She had gone too far. She knew that berating herself for her foolhardiness would do nothing to help the situation, but she just could not help it. He was deeply upset and she was the cause of that.

At the mango tree near her parents' home, Mr. Ritchie stopped and finally turned to Cassandra.

"I thank you for your company this morning, Miss Renwick." His voice was distant, but he was clearly trying to be pleasant.

She longed to reach out to him—to hold his hand, look into his eyes, and apologize profusely. She blinked a few times to clear her eyes.

She did the best she could, the only thing she could do. Extending her gloved hand to him, she replied, "Thank *you* so much, Mr. Ritchie. I greatly appreciate you taking the time to ride with me. And . . . and for answering my impertinent questions."

Mr. Ritchie's shoulders relaxed and his smile lost its forced quality and moved into his eyes. "Not at all."

Suavely, he bent over her extended hand and placed a light kiss on the back of her glove. "It was entirely my pleasure. I would be honored if we could go riding again sometime. Perhaps I could even show you some of those smaller alleyways if you are interested?"

Hope bloomed inside of her again. He had forgiven her! He understood that she had not meant to hurt him. She did not know how he knew, but he did.

"Oh, yes. I would greatly enjoy that," she said, not even trying to control the broad smile she knew was covering her face.

"I know you will not mind, Miss Renwick, telling me once again about these new colors which have become popular in London," Helena Scottsdale said, leaning closer to Cassandra.

Cassandra forced a smile to her lips and tried her best to look interested. It was not easy, since at any moment she knew that Major Vernon would be coming in.

Her mother had told her so about half a dozen times

while she breakfasted. Cassandra had lost count of the number of times she had been reminded to be warm and welcoming when he arrived, so as to make up for her anger of the previous evening.

But she did not want to be warm and welcoming to Major Vernon. She had tried to tell her mother this, but she just would not listen. She was still determined that Cassandra marry him.

Only one thing kept her from completely losing her temper with her mother—Mr. Ritchie.

She knew that if she lost her temper and said all that she was longing to say, her mother would not allow her to go out again except under her watchful eye.

And now, Cassandra wanted more than anything to see Mr. Ritchie. She was on a mission. She *would* learn more about India and Eurasians. She would do so in order to be better prepared to fight for their cause.

So now she sat here being pleasant and dreading Major Vernon's arrival when she would have to be witty and charming.

Cassandra noticed at once when he entered the room. Miss Scottsdale clearly had noted the newcomer's entrance as well for she sat up a little straighter and patted her hair to make sure every curl was in place.

Major Vernon, for his part, seemed to have come to make amends. After making his bow to her mother, he went directly to Cassandra and presented her with a large bouquet of red roses, declaring, "I do hope you will forgive me, Miss Renwick. I had no intention of offending you last evening."

Miss Scottsdale sighed audibly. Cassandra was completely taken aback by this gesture and went so far as to chastise herself for her disparaging thoughts about Major Vernon's character.

Seeing the color of the roses, however, she sincerely hoped that Major Vernon had not developed any romantic notions regarding her. She certainly felt none toward him.

But rather than provide another opportunity for her mother to get angry with her, she curtseyed and took the peace offering, murmuring, "So kind, Major Vernon. Of course, I could not stay angry with you."

Lady Renwick fluttered toward them. "Oh my, what lovely flowers. How very kind of you, Major Vernon. Why, that was entirely unnecessary, my dear sir. I don't wonder if it should not have been Cassandra who should apologize to you. How very thoughtful!"

Cassandra bit her tongue to keep a rude retort from escaping her mouth. Apologize to him indeed! He had been the one who had been horribly rude to her, laughing at her and her desire to become better acquainted with the world around her.

She kept her eyes lowered, however, so that he could not see the anger in them, and instead focused on Major Vernon's boots—until she noticed them moving away. She stole a glance up and saw him being pulled away by another eager mama to meet her simpering daughter.

Miss Scottsdale watched as the Major moved away. With her eyes still on his broad, red-coated back, she said in nearly a whisper to Cassandra, "My, my, Miss Renwick, I have never heard of Major Vernon bringing flowers or even an apology to a young lady before. And you have not even mentioned to me what happened last night. I thought we were friends!"

Cassandra had not intended for all of Calcutta society to learn of her disagreement with Major Vernon. But now they surely would. "Indeed, Miss Scottsdale, nothing untoward happened. Major Vernon happened to rub me the wrong way and I let him know my thoughts."

Cassandra gave a shrug and willed away her anger. There was no point in holding on to it, surely, for it would only get her into trouble.

She gave Miss Scottsdale a little smile and let her inner actress have free rein. "Fortunately, my mother stopped me just in time from really letting loose on him. I admit,

I had not even realized that he was aware he had hurt my sensibilities. And indeed, I did not expect this!"

Miss Scottsdale smiled a sad but knowing smile at her new friend. "Well, it is clear that Major Vernon seems to have a preference for one who speaks her mind. Although, I am sure, I would never have thought it of him."

"Nor I, Miss Scottsdale, nor I," Cassandra agreed whole-heartedly.

Was it possible that Major Vernon truly had feelings for her? She wondered if he was simply making this gesture so as not to risk her alienation. Or was he truly sorry for laughing at her? Whatever it was, it reeked of men like Lord Felbridge—too effusive in a false tone.

Cassandra tried not to scowl. She could not easily avoid this man, especially with her mother hovering over him.

Cassandra could not help but notice the frequency with which Major Vernon looked her way. After she had avoided his glance for the third time, he managed to give Mrs. Hurst the slip and sit down in the recently vacated chair next to Cassandra's.

Cassandra decided that she had to bite the bullet and feign civility. "Thank you again for the roses, Major Vernon. They, and your apology, were both very lovely, and really completely unnecessary. Indeed, I should be the one to apologize to you for allowing my tongue to get the better of me last evening."

"Not at all, Miss Renwick. I did seem to have provoked you. But," he asked incredulously, "Are you truly interested in politics and such things?"

Then, leaning forward and smiling, he continued, "I never would have believed such a pretty girl as you could be interested in such dull things."

Cassandra breathed deeply, willing herself not to get angry with this single-minded oaf. "Indeed, Major, I am interested in such things. Why is it impossible for you to believe this?"

But Cassandra's mother, spying their tête-à-tête, intruded quickly before Major Vernon had a chance to comprehend her barb.

"Tell me, Major Vernon, do you intend on being present at the assembly next Tuesday evening? It was such a sad crush last month that I am tempted not to go at all next week, but to hold a little gathering here instead." Lady Renwick gestured around the room as if her 'little' gathering could fit in the drawing room.

"Certainly it will not be as large as Cassandra's coming-out ball," she continued, "but just some of our closer friends for a little music and dancing. What do you think?"

"What an excellent scheme, Lady Renwick!" Major Vernon immediately fell in with his hostess's plan. "I completely agree with you about the assembly. They seem to be getting less and less discriminating about who they let in, rather than more. Why, I even saw that they had given vouchers to some Eurasians! I was quite shocked."

"As was I, dear Major, as was I. It is quite disgraceful, to be sure." Lady Renwick gave a look to Cassandra as if to say *I told you so*.

Cassandra bit her tongue until it hurt.

As the Major and Lady Renwick chatted amiably, Cassandra looked more closely at him and wondered what had made him so bigoted. She then looked at her mother and wondered the same thing about her.

She would never become like them, never.

Their bigotry seemed rather like a disease that infected one the longer one stayed in Calcutta. Was her father the same way, she wondered? She did not think so, but she would need to speak with him to find out.

She was jerked out of her reverie by her mother, who was saying, "A drive tomorrow afternoon sounds lovely, does it not, Cassandra?"

"Hmm? Tomorrow afternoon? Oh, no, I am sorry, Major Vernon, I already have an engagement tomorrow afternoon."

"With whom? This is the first I have heard of it," said her mother with a touch of irritation.

"I am to go shopping with Gisela Brown. Did I not mention it to you? I am so sorry!" she invented quickly. Then, turning to Major Vernon, she added, "Mrs. Brown was so kind as to chaperone me on my journey here from England. I would just hate to disappoint her. You will forgive me and allow us to go for a ride the following day, will you not?"

This was so sweetly said that even Lady Renwick was mollified. Major Vernon sketched her a bow. "Of course. You ladies and your shopping expeditions! I know that they are quite important."

"Oh, indeed, they are!" Cassandra agreed briefly, already beginning to think about how she could wipe that chauvinistic smile off his face. But then remembering her real reason for dissembling—the drive into the mysterious narrow lanes of Calcutta promised by Mr. Ritchie—she held her tongue and proceeded to be uncharacteristically docile for the rest of the morning.

She could not risk her mother finding out the truth.

Julian was holding the reins so tightly that his hands were cramping. If only Miss Renwick did not have to sit quite so close to him! But with the addition of her maid, there was very little space on the phaeton's bench. It really was not made to hold more than two people.

Fire licked at Julian's blood, heating it to distraction. He could feel the length of Miss Renwick's creamy white arm brushing against his and her knee bumping up against him.

He should not feel this way. His conscience screamed at him and told his body to calm itself.

He was here to woo her so that she fell in love with him. That was all.

There were to be no reciprocal feelings. None.

He saw that Miss Renwick's eyes were slipping toward

him with a pleasing frequency. She was just as aware of him as he was of her.

That was good. That was as it should be.

Was there anything else he could do, or should do, to promote this attraction? He tried to think of it in an abstract way, but instead his body flamed once again as she raised her arm to brush a lovely golden curl from her face and gave him a shy smile in the process.

Julian concentrated on his driving. It needed his full attention now, for the streets were becoming more crowded as they moved away from the English section of town.

"Mr. Ritchie, tell me a little of what we are going to see," Miss Renwick asked so quietly that he had to bend towards her a bit.

Her hair smelled wonderful! She smelled like roses and jasmine. He must get another opportunity to get close to her.

Wait, she had asked him a question. What had she asked? Oh yes, about what they would be seeing. My goodness, he had to keep focused!

"I am simply going to drive down some of the streets in the older sections of Calcutta, Miss Renwick. What you will see is simply life in India as it is lived by the Bengalis."

"Is it the way you live?"

Julian felt his heart grow cold.

Was she going to probe him again? He had hoped that she had finished with her inquisitiveness after their ride. She had seemed so sad after he had taken offense at her questions. But now it seemed that she was going to do the same thing again.

What was it that she wanted—to bare his soul? To delve into the most painful experiences of his life?

Why did she want to hurt him this way?

"I am sorry, Mr. Ritchie. I suppose it is very wrong of me to ask such personal questions of you."

Well, she had interpreted his silence correctly, he acknowledged with surprise.

"I do live in a traditional Bengali house because my

mother is Bengali," he said, hoping that that would be enough to satisfy her.

"But your father is not."

Julian felt his hands grip the reins tightly once again, but now it was his anger that was on a short leash.

"Miss Renwick, why do you persist in asking such questions?" he said, trying his best to keep his voice steady and calm.

"I am terribly sorry." She took a deep shuddering breath. He could feel it through her body. If he were not so angry with her prying, he would have been very tempted to put his arms around her—to hold her and comfort her.

"I do not mean to upset you," she said. "It is just that . . . well, I thought that if I learned more about you and the way you live and grew up—the way you have been treated and still are treated by the English—that I might . . . I might do something to help you."

"Help me? How could you help me?" His chest began to loosen again.

"I am not entirely sure. Perhaps I could speak with the governor-general, or with people in society. I want to do something, Mr. Ritchie. It is not right, the way people cut you. It is not your fault your parents are from different cultures. And you should not have to pay the price for it."

Her voice had grown more steady as she had warmed to her cause and in turn it warmed him.

She wanted to help him.

Julian almost laughed. Little did she know it, but she was indeed going to help him. She was going to help him get revenge on the people who had hurt him the most—her own parents.

But he could not tell her that. He could not let her know of his plan.

7

"That is very . . . thoughtful of you, Miss Renwick. I appreciate your sentiments, but truly you do not need to do this." Mr. Ritchie drew his brows down in concern, but continued to look ahead at where he was driving. Cassandra just could not concentrate on their interesting surroundings, however—she was too intent on her argument.

"But I do! If I do not, then nothing will change," she said vehemently.

"Even if you do try, still, nothing may change."

She did not say anything, but just looked blindly out at the street in front of them.

Was he right? Was what she was trying to do impossible?

Cassandra suddenly felt at a loss. All of her wonderful plans and ideas to change the way people treated this poor man—were they for nothing?

Mr. Ritchie turned to her as much as was possible while still driving. "Perhaps, if you truly want to do something, Miss Renwick, you can learn more about India and encourage other Englishmen to do the same. At least then there may be some understanding instead of just blind prejudice."

Cassandra turned back towards Mr. Ritchie, struck by his words.

"Look about you, Miss Renwick," Mr. Ritchie continued,

"India is a fascinating place. Although I have never been to England, I have read a great deal about it, and I know that there is nothing like this there." He motioned with his hand at the street before them.

Indeed, it was like nothing Cassandra had ever seen before. Men wearing long shirts and lengths of cloth loosely wrapped around their limbs walked down the street purposefully, some carrying huge heavy baskets filled with fruit or vegetables. Women in brightly colored saris filled large brass urns at street-side wells and then disappeared into narrow doors.

It *was* fascinating. Cassandra wondered if her mother had ever driven through this part of Calcutta before. She strongly suspected that she had not. She kept to her own world and tried to make that as English as she could.

A loud braying sound caught Cassandra's attention as a large, hump-backed cow was forced to move out of the way of Mr. Ritchie's phaeton. The men walking past, carrying the baskets of goods on their heads, called out their wares. Cassandra could not understand what they said, but it sounded very much like a song. It was actually a lovely cacophony of sound all around them.

And beside her, Mr. Ritchie's strong arm held firm onto the reins. She could imagine that same arm encircling her—holding her with strength and comfort, but gently.

She felt his warmth, sitting as close to him as she was. And when he leaned down to hear what she said, he smelled so wonderful—of sandalwood and soap. She had deliberately spoken softly a few times just so that he would have to bend toward her to hear what she was saying.

It was all very wrong, especially since she wasn't even interested in men—not even the exotic and attractive Julian Ritchie.

But she just could not help it. Just sitting next to him made her feel good.

A man passed by, walking quickly with a huge load of vegetables in the basket on his head. Cassandra was forced to exclaim, "My goodness, look at all that man is carrying!"

"I am sorry, Miss Renwick, who?" Mr. Ritchie's mind seemed to have been elsewhere.

Maybe he too had been having thoughts along the same lines as her own.

"That man who just passed us. He has such a heavy basket on his head! Surely he does not think he can sell all that while walking the streets."

"Oh no. He is going to the bazaar."

"Oh, how I would love to see that," Cassandra said. She was beginning to think that perhaps Mr. Ritchie was right, and she should explore more of native India.

Especially, her heart said treacherously, if it meant being with him.

"I would be happy to take you one day," he offered, just as she had hoped he would.

Cassandra's heart gave a leap.

Gisela Brown had not minded playing Cassandra's alibi for today. But would she mind doing so again?

Cassandra twirled around, her hand held securely in Major Vernon's. Dancing was the one thing that made coming to these parties bearable. She did love to dance.

"Have I told you, Miss Renwick, how lovely that color is on you?" Major Vernon asked as they promenaded down the line. "It brings out the roses in your cheeks and makes your beautiful blue eyes shine."

Cassandra laughed to herself at his effusive compliments. He was forever saying such ridiculous things—it quite reminded her of Lord Felbridge.

In fact, Lord Felbridge's compliments were exactly what had first attracted her to him. But now she knew better and Major Vernon's praises left her untouched and even annoyed at times.

"You are doing it too brown, Major. It is simply the

dancing that has put color into my cheeks and the sparkle in my eye."

"And you are a very graceful dancer. I am always honored when you stand up with me," was his quick reply.

Luckily, the movements of the dance made it impossible for them to further this useless conversation. Much more of it, and Cassandra knew she would entirely lose her joy of the dance.

Her next dance partner was not quite as adept at flowery compliments, and for that Cassandra was grateful. Reggie White was a pleasant, understated gentleman. He rather reminded Cassandra of old St. Nick with his round belly and rosy cheeks.

He was also always a very happy person, filled with meaningless prattle that made Cassandra laugh. She was still giggling after their dance ended and he returned her to her mama.

"Thank you so much, Mr. White. I do always enjoy dancing with you," Cassandra said while curtseying.

He bowed in return. "It is entirely my pleasure."

It was then that Mr. Ritchie walked up to them, boldly ignoring the glare from Cassandra's mother.

Cassandra felt her heart begin to beat faster. She gave him a broad, welcoming smile as he approached.

Mr. Ritchie was carrying two glasses of lemonade. Offering one to Cassandra and the other to her mother, he said, "Good evening, Lady Renwick. Miss Renwick, you looked in need of some refreshment."

"Thank you, sir. I could not be more grateful. It is quite warm this evening, is it not?" Cassandra tried to behave normally, but just seeing Mr. Ritchie here had brightened her entire evening.

"Indeed. It is a trifle warm for November, wouldn't you agree, Reggie?" Mr. Ritchie said, turning to the other gentleman.

"Yes, rather," he answered, giving Mr. Ritchie a quizzical look.

"I believe you are correct, Mr. White, it is unusually

warm," Lady Renwick said. "I am certain Major Vernon would be happy to escort you for a stroll around the garden, Cassandra. If you will excuse us, gentlemen."

"Oh, but Mama, I am certain Mr. Ritchie would be happy to do the same, would you not, sir?" Cassandra asked, smiling encouragingly at him.

"I would be honored," Mr. Ritchie said quickly.

Her mother scowled. "Yes, well, we will not impose upon you further, Mr. Ritchie."

She handed him back her empty lemonade glass as if he were a servant.

"It would be no imposition at all, I assure you, ma'am."

"My daughter should be escorted by one of her peers, Mr. Ritchie, not you."

With this parting shot, Lady Renwick turned her back on the gentleman and practically dragged Cassandra away.

Cassandra had never been more embarrassed. In one moment her mother had completely spoiled her good mood. "Mother, how could you?" she said as soon as she could find her voice.

"What do you mean, how could I? I did only what should be done—I put that young man firmly in his place," her mother said, looking around Mrs. Hurst's ballroom for Major Vernon

"But that is not right. He is my peer! And if he is not, it is because he is a better person than I, for he is able to deal with people like you."

"Nonsense. You do not know what you are talking about," her mother said dismissively.

Lady Renwick's voice brightened. "Ah, there he is." She waved her fan in Major Vernon's direction. He was speaking with another young lady, but at Lady Renwick's summons, he abandoned her and immediately joined them.

Her mother gave the officer her most beguiling smile. "Major, my poor daughter is quite overheated after all that dancing. Would you be so kind as to take her for a stroll though the gardens?"

Major Vernon's face lit up at the suggestion. He bowed to Cassandra, saying, "I would be more than honored to do so."

"Well, I would not. I do not mean to be rude, sir, but I am not interested in going for a walk," Cassandra said, her ire making her much more direct than usual.

"Cassandra, do not be silly. You just said that you were very warm and would be happy to go for a stroll."

"Yes, when I was speaking with Mr. Ritchie. Now, however, I am feeling perfectly well again and have no need to go outside. Thank you very much, Major."

As Cassandra began to turn her back on the gentleman, her mother grabbed her wrist.

"Do not be rude, my girl," her mother said, her eyes piercing into Cassandra's.

Cassandra knew she was in trouble, but there was nothing for it now. She was not going to allow her mother to browbeat her into going for a walk with Major Vernon when she would have much preferred Mr. Ritchie's company.

Truth be told, Major Vernon reminded her too often of Lord Felbridge.

"It is of no consequence, Lady Renwick. If Miss Renwick does not wish to walk in the garden with me, I shall survive, perhaps . . ." he allowed his voice to trail off and gave her the saddest expression.

Cassandra could not help but laugh. He looked like a lost little puppy dog. "Oh, very well, Major Vernon, I will walk with you."

He immediately perked up. "Good. I could not stand the thought that I'd been put out by a half-breed."

He put out his arm for Cassandra to take, but she had frozen at his comment.

"How dare you! Mr. Ritchie is ten times the man you are. He is kind and considerate and, and . . . Oh!"

Cassandra had never been so furious in her life. She stormed away from both her mother and Major Vernon. She didn't know where she was going, but she knew she needed to get away from such horrible condescending, bigoted people.

How could he? How dare he?

She ran out of the room and stormed through the garden, whacking at helpless bushes with her fan, not keeping to the paths which were lined with pretty colored lanterns. She stomped across the well-manicured lawn.

Finally, when she reached the outside wall, she was forced to stop. Her breath was coming fast and her heart pounded in anger.

"It is not worth it," a quiet voice just behind her said.

She spun around to see Mr. Ritchie standing there in the dark, his white smile standing out even more than usual against his brown face.

Cassandra leaned back against the wall and looked up at the millions of stars above them. Blinking back her tears of anger, she said, "It is just so unfair! How can they treat you so?"

She stood up again and looked directly at him. "How can you just stand there and take such rudeness? *Why* do you take it?"

Mr. Ritchie shrugged. "I suppose I am used to it. Besides, what am I going to do? What could I possibly do to make them stop?"

He came forward, and then turned his back and leaned against the wall as she had just done.

Crossing his arms over his chest, he said, "I used to think that being just like them would make me acceptable. I can out-English any Englishman without even thinking about it. My English is impeccable, I play cricket and ride—and yet still my skin refuses to turn white.

"And while it is still brown I will be looked down upon, no matter what I do."

Cassandra's heart felt like a stone weighing down inside her chest. "Don't you get upset by this?"

"I used to. Now I get angry. Very angry," he said so quietly that a shiver of fear ran through Cassandra.

There was an awkward silence.

"It's just not fair. It's not right," Cassandra whispered, her voice refusing to cooperate as she held back her tears. "People should just accept you for who you are."

Mr. Ritchie laughed. It was a sad, hollow laugh with no amusement in it at all. "In a perfect world, Miss Renwick. Not in this one."

He stood up and moved forward, gently taking her arm. "Come, let me escort you back to the ball. You should not be out here for too long. Your mother will get worried."

She allowed him to walk with her back to the house. As they strolled down the path, Cassandra wracked her mind for some way in which she could help him.

"Have you thought that if you dressed more fashionably, people would accept you more readily?" she asked hesitantly.

"I have tried that," he admitted with a little laugh. "Like everything else, it didn't really make a difference. I would prefer to be accepted for who I am, not how I am dressed."

Cassandra nodded her head, certain that he was right. If he was not accepted because of the color of his skin, just changing his clothes shouldn't make a difference.

They slowed before they got to the more populated areas of the garden.

"Won't you come in with me, Mr. Ritchie?" Cassandra asked when he stopped walking.

"No. It would not do for it to become known that we were out here alone. You go ahead."

Cassandra nodded sadly, knowing that he spoke the truth.

"Oh, Miss Renwick," he said, stopping her before she got too far.

He quickly caught up with her. "Do not forget our outing to the bazaar on Saturday," he said quietly, just in case anyone else was nearby.

Now this was the first happy thought Cassandra had

had for much of the evening. Not that she had forgotten for one moment about the long-awaited outing.

How could she? It was what she was looking forward to more than anything.

As Cassandra was searching through her wardrobe on Friday afternoon, looking for just the right dress to wear to the bazaar, Gita asked hesitantly, "Miss, would you be interested in wearing a sari?"

Cassandra whirled around to face her ayah. "A sari? I would love to! But I do not own one."

"I would be happy to lend you one of mine," Gita offered.

"Would you? Would it fit me?" Cassandra was beginning to get very excited, but she was a good four inches taller than her maid and thinner as well.

Gita laughed gently. "Oh, yes, Miss. Saris only come in one size. They fit everybody."

"That would be wonderful! Oh, I can just imagine Mr. Ritchie's expression when he sees me in a sari!" Cassandra said, clapping her hands together.

"I am not suggesting this to impress Mr. Ritchie." Gita looked rather serious.

Cassandra looked at her maid skeptically. "Then why are you suggesting it?"

"Because it is not proper for a young English lady to go to an Indian bazaar. Even girls from good Indian families do not go to the bazaar. It is just not done."

Gita held her hand up as Cassandra was about to protest. "I know that you will not be turned from your desire to go, Miss, but that is why I want you to blend in with the other people there as much as possible. It is for your own safety."

Cassandra realized then just how lucky she was to have such an understanding maid. Instinctively, she gave Gita a hug. "You are very good to me, Gita."

The maid extracted herself quickly, but could neither

hide the smile on her face nor the tears in her eyes. "I will bring you the sari tomorrow, Miss."

Cassandra had the good sense to leave her parents' house in her usual dress and to then change her clothing at Gisela's. She knew she would have to pass a number of people just to leave, and any one of them might mention her unusual dress to her mother.

Gita had brought along one of her best saris for the occasion. After the ayah had finished the complicated winding and pleating of the sari, Cassandra stared at her reflection in the cheval glass.

She was almost unrecognizable! The woman who stared back at her looked exotic and, dare she even think it, sensuous.

The brilliant blue silk sari clung to her curves, accentuating her figure even as it concealed it. The gold thread that had been used to embroider delicate flowers all along the border of the sari glinted as it picked up the highlights in her own golden hair. For modesty, though, Gita instructed Cassandra to cover her head and part of her face with the tail of the sari, showing her how to hold the end so that it would not slip off.

At four o'clock sharp, she met Mr. Ritchie, who was waiting for her in his phaeton on the street corner outside Gisela's house.

At first, he looked right past her. Even when she stopped directly in front of him, he stared dumbly at her for a moment. Then, with an incredulous smile, he jumped down to greet her.

"Miss Renwick? I almost did not recognize you! You look so, so . . ."

"Indian? Strange?" Cassandra met his smile with a shy one of her own.

"Ravishing! Beautiful!" Mr. Ritchie finally finished, his cheeks flushing a deep red. He suddenly found the ground in front of him very interesting.

Cassandra giggled, but then tried to look up at him demurely from under the end of the sari covering her blond tresses.

"Thank you. It was my ayah's idea that I dress this way, so that I would not look too out of place at the bazaar. I see that you are also wearing native clothes, perhaps for the same reason?"

Mr. Ritchie was, indeed, dressed as many Indian men in a long, fine shirt of a pastel blue, with delicate white embroidery around the collar and down the front. This was paired with tight white muslin pants that sheathed his muscular calves like a second skin. Freed from his dated English clothing, he looked exotic and breathtakingly masculine.

Cassandra felt herself tingle with anticipation. She felt her heart beat faster as he helped her first up into his phaeton, followed by Gita.

Cassandra was lured by his tantalizing scent to lean toward him as they began to make their way through the narrow streets. As always, he smelled so clean and yet with a hint of spice that was so pleasant to inhale.

They drove straight to the street where the local bazaar was held, but the traffic became so congested that they soon had to abandon their conveyance and proceed on foot like most other people.

Despite her dress, Cassandra received not a few stares as she slowly walked next to Mr. Ritchie, amazed at all of the brilliant colors and unusual things that were for sale. Gita walked as closely behind her as she could without stepping on her heels.

The street was crowded with people slowly walking up and down inspecting the fruits that the food sellers had carefully piled on large banana leaves on the ground. Cassandra crouched down on the ground in front of one and picked up a fruit she did not recognize. It was large and green with splashes of orange.

"That is a papaya," Mr. Ritchie explained. "They can be very sweet."

Cassandra replaced the papaya and then asked about a pyramid of round green fruit.

Again Mr. Ritchie explained, "Those are raw guava. They can be tart, but are very refreshing on a hot day."

The fruit seller sat and stared at Cassandra as if she had just descended from the sky while she asked Mr. Ritchie about all of the unfamiliar fruits.

But as she stood up to leave, his brows shot up and he said something to them in Bengali.

"He wants to know if you want to buy anything," Gita translated for her.

Cassandra had not thought of buying anything, but now an idea occurred to her. It would be a nice thank you gift for Gisela to present her with some of the more exotic fruit. She nodded and pointed to the papaya.

Gita immediately stepped forward and began bargaining with the man. After some tough negotiations which involved Gita turning away twice, the man finally relented and sold four different types of fruit to them for what Gita seemed to consider a reasonable price.

As they watched other people negotiate for goods, Mr. Ritchie leaned down toward Cassandra. "Are you sure you do not want to leave, Miss Renwick? Are you truly interested in seeing all of the market? It is rather dirty."

"Oh, no, Mr. Ritchie, I do not mind the dirt. I am finding it absolutely fascinating. Is there more to see?"

He laughed at her enthusiasm and led them on to another section where vegetables were on display in the same manner as the fruit had been.

This time Cassandra realized that she should stand back and look from afar.

Pointing to the different types of vegetables, she asked Mr. Ritchie once again to tell her the names of all of the unfamiliar ones.

This time, however, he was unable to identify many of the vegetables she pointed to. He shook his head and laughed. "I am afraid that, although I have probably eaten all of these vegetables, I have never seen them raw. When they are given to me, they are cut and cooked."

Cassandra smiled, understanding at once. She turned to Gita for help. Unfortunately, Gita only knew the names of the vegetables in Bengali. But between the two of them, Mr. Ritchie and Gita were able to identify and describe each one to her.

A little farther down the road, they were assailed by the sharp smell of fish.

Once again, Mr. Ritchie stopped and asked Cassandra if she would rather leave, but once again she insisted that they go on, despite the terrible smells.

As they entered a large area that was the fish market, Gita handed Cassandra a handkerchief scented with perfume that she had brought for the purpose. Fish, being the staple of the Bengali diet, had the largest space in the bazaar.

It was, however, also the dirtiest section of the market, with scales littering the floor and splashes of dirty water from the fish that were still alive and swimming in the small containers in front of the fishmongers.

Cassandra did not insist on staying there long, for the smell was overwhelming.

When the party returned to Clive Street, Mr. Ritchie helped the two women down from his phaeton outside the gates to her father's house.

Cassandra felt his smile all the way down to her toes. "Now I shall have to think up another interesting outing for you."

"I should like that very much!" Cassandra said. "I am truly enjoying learning about Calcutta and its people. You are a wonderful tour guide," she laughed, meaning for him to take her comment as a joke.

But he just stood there smiling down at her with a look in his eyes that made Cassandra's knees go weak.

"Well, good-bye, then," he said, not moving.

"Good-bye." The end of her sari slipped off of her head.

She let go of it so that she could take the hand that he held out to her.

If perhaps he held her hand a little too long for propriety, she did not notice. She was too caught up by the contrast of his jet-black hair and his stunning blue eyes, set off by his honeyed-brown skin.

Gita's cough interrupted the spell. He dropped her hand abruptly and smiled a rather embarrassed smile at the ayah. Cassandra felt herself blush and looked down.

"Thank you, again," she said quietly. She then turned and rushed through the gates and into the house, the end of her sari flying behind her.

Running to her room, Cassandra released the breath she seemed to have been holding without realizing it. She stood, slightly dazed, as Gita unwound the sari and dressed her in a sprigged muslin gown.

Her excitement of the trip to the bazaar was replaced by a completely different type of exhilaration—a fire sparked by those intense blue eyes.

For a girl who had determined never to feel anything for any man ever again, her desire to be with Mr. Ritchie was very disconcerting. She had tried to fight it, and she knew that she should continue to do so.

But it was getting more difficult by the day to ignore these feelings.

Cassandra idly wondered what her mother would say if she knew that she had held Mr. Ritchie's hand and wanted to do so again. His hands were so large and strong, yet he had held hers ever so gently.

Her mother would be shocked, horrified even, if she found out about Cassandra's outings. And yet, Cassandra just could not reconcile her mother's prejudiced ideas with the reality of Mr. Ritchie.

8

As soon as he entered his house, Julian slipped off the Indian sandals that he had worn to the bazaar. Feeling tired from all the walking he had done and hungry from all the food they had looked at, he went in search of his mother.

His conscience still pricked him about how he had held Miss Renwick's hand before they parted, but something inside of him just did not want to let her go.

Perhaps it was seeing her in that sari, or her enthusiasm and interest in the most mundane of outings? Whatever it was, he had to remind himself of why he was deliberately spending time with her.

Yes, she was an interesting girl, although she did ask the most outrageous and bold questions anyone had ever asked him. And it could not be denied that she was beautiful enough to set his blood pounding through his body.

But he was bent on revenge, he sternly reminded himself. He would make Lady Renwick pay for all the years of torment she had put him through.

He did not care for Miss Renwick—he cared only to teach her bigoted mother a lesson in humanity and humility.

Julian had repeated this argument to himself nearly every night as he lay in his bed, Miss Renwick's lovely blue eyes and sweet angelic face swimming before his eyes. He could not afford to lose sight of his intentions. Otherwise things could become very dangerous.

He found his mother supervising the cooking of his dinner in the open courtyard in the center of their house.

"Oh, there you are, Ma."

"Have you been looking for me?" his mother asked, smiling up at her son.

"Yes, is dinner ready? I am exceedingly hungry today," he replied, after properly touching her feet with respect.

"I am just seeing to it. It should be ready in a few minutes. You wash up and I shall see to the setting of the dining table for you."

"No need to do that. I will eat on the floor, Indian style," he said, moving away to get cleaned up.

After washing away the grime of the bazaar, Julian changed his white pants for a more comfortable lungi. Still tying the floor-length cloth around his waist so that it fell like a skirt from his narrow hips, he went into the dining room.

As he ate, his mother asked, "Where have you been this afternoon?"

"I took a friend to the bazaar," he answered, unsure of whether he should admit to his mother who that friend was. He remembered her admonition not to see Miss Renwick, and did not want to hurt his mother by showing his direct disobedience.

"Really? Who is this who would want to go to an Indian bazaar?" she asked.

"Oh, just an English fellow in my office. He is new to Calcutta and said he would like to get to know the country in which he is now living."

Julian paused, feeling terrible about lying to his mother. "I think it is very admirable."

His mother smiled, "Admirable, yes, but most unusual."

"Yes, that is why I am happy to take him around. Can

you think of any other places that he might be interested in seeing?" Julian asked.

His mother thought for a few moments and then answered slowly, "Your father was also very interested in seeing more of native India. My father took him to the ruins of the Shiva temple just south of Calcutta. I believe he enjoyed it a great deal."

"To the Shiva temple?" Julian stopped to think about it. He had not been there for many years. If he was not mistaken, the outside of the temple was decorated with sculptures that had been inspired by the writings in the Kama Sutra, the Indian book of love.

A smile slowly crept over Julian's face. That would be a perfect place to take Miss Renwick! Why had he not thought of that himself?

Of course, a temple of love would be a perfect place to inspire romance. He would have her swooning over him in no time.

He sat back with the smile still on his face, wondering when he should plan this outing and just how he was going to pull it off.

In the back of his mind, he also wondered just what the proper Lady Renwick would say if she knew that the unworthy Julian Ritchie was going to take her sweet, innocent daughter to see sculptures of naked people doing unspeakable acts.

Julian looked up as Miss Renwick entered her father's library.

"Good afternoon, Miss Renwick. I hope you are well?" he said, attempting to sound as if nothing was out of the ordinary—as if they hadn't just had the most wonderful time together the previous day and as if he didn't want to stride over to her, take her in his arms and kiss her soundly.

"Oh! I am sorry, Mr. Ritchie. I did not know you were here. I did not mean to disturb you. I will not be more than a minute. I just wanted to get the next volume of this book I am reading." Miss Renwick spoke quickly, trying to hide the smile that came to her face.

If Julian didn't know better, he would think that she could read his mind. No, if she knew what he was thinking, her beautiful face would be bright red.

Julian hid his own smile and watched as she slowly scanned the shelves pretending to look for another book, while actually stealing very meaningful glances in his direction.

When she had finally found the volume she had been looking for, he said, "Miss Renwick, I do not know if it can be arranged, but if you are interested, there are some fascinating and beautiful ruins of an ancient Hindu temple not so very far away. It is about a two hour ride to the south."

"Oh, that sounds fascinating!" she said in all eagerness.

A white owl abruptly flew in through the open window behind Julian. The owl's wing grazed his head, disturbing his carefully arranged locks. It then circled the room, finally alighting on top of a bookcase.

Miss Renwick had let out a startled scream when the bird had flown in. Now Julian motioned to her to be calm and quiet so as not to scare the bird.

He then slowly walked to the door and began to close it, calling softly for a servant to come quickly with something to catch a bird.

A few minutes later, the door slowly crept open. The elderly servant, Promeela, came into the room and carefully closed the door behind her.

Miss Renwick's eyes widened in fright at the sight of the woman. She looked ancient, with lines creasing every part of her face. Her beaked nose protruded sharply from her long, thin face, which ended in a pointed chin.

The old woman, completely ignoring Julian and Miss Renwick, took a quick look around the room in order to locate the bird. Spotting it on the bookcase, she followed the owl's line of sight and saw Julian, standing near the desk.

The old hag let out a cackle of laughter that was very loud in the silent room. She spoke in Bengali, but it was unclear to whom she was speaking, as she was looking directly at the bird.

"Oh Ma! This one has been blessed. The way you stare at him so, Ma, he will surely bear your blessings for his life. Wealthy beyond his dreams!" the old woman cackled.

Julian froze. Wealthy beyond his dreams! The bird *had* touched him when it had flown into the window and now it sat and gazed at him. It was rather unnerving the way it stared, unblinking.

Could it be true? Could he be destined to become rich? If he were wealthy, no one would shun him as they did now. He would have the status that came with riches, and people would accept him despite his heritage.

How lovely would that be—to have what he had wanted all of his life. He didn't so much care for the money, only for what it would give him—the social acceptance.

The old woman looked at him sideways. "You understand me, Englishman?" she crooned.

It was clear that the old woman had not realized that he would understand her. Despite his coloring, she thought him to be English.

He had been tempted to let her continue to think that, but the ridiculous nature of her statement had caught him off-guard, and he supposed his expression had given him away.

"I am only half-English," he explained in the native tongue. "My mother is Bengali."

"Oh Baba," the old woman came toward him, her toothless grin wide on her face, "you can spare some sweets for an old woman. You are going to be rich." She held her gnarly hand out and looked up at him, waiting for her tip.

Julian looked at her pleading face and thought of the

money he had in his pocket. It was just enough to buy a cup of tea and a few sweets for himself in the afternoon.

No matter how much an owl stared at him, it did not put money into his pocket.

"Just get the bird and get out, woman. Stop spouting your nonsense!" Julian said, more harshly than he had intended.

The old woman is a fool as well as a witch, he thought to himself. *And I am an even bigger fool to be taken in by her superstitions.*

He had never met Promeela before, but her reputation for being a witch was well-known among the servants and the local native community. They all came to her for her potions, for she could cure nearly anything with her herbs.

But he had never heard that she could prophesy.

He then noticed Miss Renwick looking at him, her mouth open in surprise. If he hadn't been so embarrassed, he would have been tempted to laugh at her expression.

She quickly closed her mouth, blushing when she saw him looking at her.

"The old woman is spouting old mythical nonsense," he told Miss Renwick by way of explanation.

"What did she say?"

Julian shrugged his shoulders and smiled apologetically. "The white owl represents one of the goddesses in the Hindu religion—Lakshmi, the goddess of wealth. The old woman said that because the bird is looking at me, she will bestow great wealth upon me. Pure nonsense, I am sure."

Miss Renwick laughed, somehow relieving the moment of its tension. "Oh, but it would be wonderful if she is right!"

Julian did not get an opportunity to respond. While they were talking, Promeela had made cooing noises and enticed the bird to fly down to the floor. Gently picking it up, she carried the bird carefully to Julian and put it right into his face.

"You take a good look, Ma. Do not forget our friend of mixed blood who speaks our tongue. You bring him his money, and maybe he will remember old Promeela who foretold it."

Julian moved away from the bird and said sharply to the woman, "Enough of your nonsense, you old witch. Go!"

This set the woman laughing harder, but she let the bird loose out of the window and then left the room to return to work.

After Promeela was gone, Miss Renwick smiled shyly at Julian. "I did not know you spoke the native language. It is very beautiful."

"Thank you. My mother taught me."

"I suppose I assumed that you did not speak it because your English is flawless."

"I only went to English schools. But my mother speaks both languages and made sure that I did as well."

They were silent for a few moments.

Abruptly returning to their previous conversation, Julian said, "But we must think and figure out how exactly to arrange our outing, if you understand what I mean?"

"Yes, yes indeed. I will have to think about it. Will you be here again soon so that we may make arrangements? Let me see . . . today is Monday. . . ." Cassandra thought out loud. "Perhaps we can arrange for our outing on Friday?"

"I will have to switch my day off, but that should not be too difficult. I will arrange to be here at this same time the day after tomorrow so that we can discuss it further. Would that be all right?"

Miss Renwick smiled and nodded. Julian watched her as she left the office, her book clutched to her chest and a spring in her step.

* * *

Cassandra forced a smile on to her face. "Your performance was wonderful, Miss Mackley." She then gracefully congratulated the other performers and moved away from the crowd surrounding them.

Cassandra wished to go home. This had to be the most insipid entertainment ever. When her mother had told her that they were to attend a musicale by some very talented performers, she had hoped that the young ladies performing would in fact have some talent. Unfortunately, that had not been the case.

Although she did not, herself, profess to having any extraordinary musical talent, she did have a discerning ear, which was why it was painful for her to listen to her own attempts at the pianoforte. She, therefore, played as little as possible.

However, to be forced to sit and smile for two hours listening to the most pitiful performances was almost too much to ask of her. Now that it was over, she was more than ready to go home. She could feel the beginnings of a headache already.

"Oh no, Cassandra, what *can* you be thinking? We cannot leave yet! Why that would be most rude of us, to be sure," her mother had said when she had broached the subject with her.

Cassandra sighed. She had not been entirely surprised by Lady Renwick's answer, since Cassandra had interrupted her mother in the midst of a serious exchange of information with Mrs. Hurst.

Perhaps, Cassandra thought, a glass of ratafia and a breath of fresh air would help her aching head.

She took a glass as it was offered by a servant and then moved over to the open doors which led out onto a balcony. It was pleasantly cool outside, and Cassandra simply could not resist the pull of the fresh scents from the garden. The smell of Indian flowers was one thing that she could never tire of.

As she stood in the semi-darkness off in one corner of the balcony, a familiar voice wafted up to her from below.

"I must say, I could not have planned it better if I had tried. Lady Renwick is practically throwing the chit right into my lap! If she could have us leg-shackled tomorrow, I think she would do it."

A chorus of men's laughter echoed Major Vernon's voice.

"Honestly Vernon, you are the luckiest dog! Sir Lionel's daughter! You'll be set for life," another gentleman said.

"Not only do I stand an excellent chance of obtaining a rather decent position in the government, but I understand her dowry is at least five thousand pounds."

There were murmurs of appreciation from the men.

"And all you have to do is stand there, toss a few compliments the girl's way and she throws herself at your feet. I say, I wish I had such luck," Lieutenant Marcus said.

"A sweet little thing, ripe for plucking, she is," Captain Lord MacDougal added to the sniggers of the other men.

"Thank God she isn't an antidote! Don't know that I could have done it if she were," Major Vernon's voice said.

"Oh come, for a position in the government and that dowry? You could have come up to scratch."

"Well, perhaps. Oh, well, yes, I could have. Who cares what she looks like?" He began laughing harder. "She could even look like Miss Prattlesworth and I would marry her."

The men appreciated this sentiment, guffawing at the idea. After a moment, Major Vernon added more seriously, "I do hope she gets rid of that idiotic giggle though!"

"All girls have that. She'll lose it—m'sister did soon as she started having babies," Lieutenant Marcus said consolingly.

"Got to get working on your nursery quick," another man said to a round of hysterical laughter.

"I can assure you, gentleman, there will be no hesitation in that arena," Major Vernon said, laughing.

"Charge ahead, man, bayonet at the ready!"

Cassandra quickly ducked back into the house, followed by the men's hysterical laughter. She had heard enough. There was no need to put herself through any more torture tonight.

Her head was truly pounding now. She desperately hoped that her mother had finished her conversation.

Later, as Cassandra stood impatiently while Gita unbuttoned her dress, the sound of the men's laughter still echoed in her ears.

Why had she ever allowed her mother to bully her into attending such amusements? Why had she not listened to her own sound judgment and stayed at home? She would never have been subjected to such humiliation.

It was torture standing still while her corset was untied. She wanted to be moving, pacing, screaming, crying, anything but standing quietly, her emotions tied up inside of her.

Gisela had tried to tell her that all men were not the same, but here was proof at hand that in fact they were.

They all had only two things on their minds, worldly position and bedding women.

She shrugged into her night rail. "Thank you, Gita, I will brush out my hair. Good night."

Gita gave her a little bow with her hands respectfully pressed together and then quietly closed the door behind her as she left the room.

Lord Felbridge had position; he had wanted her kisses. She had merely been a toy in his hands, a lowly nothing for him to play with.

Major Vernon had thought to get both from her in one swoop.

But she wasn't having any of it. Hell would freeze over before she married Major Vernon, or any other man for that matter.

She tore the pins from her hair, happily destroying the beautiful creation Gita had arranged earlier that evening.

Dragging her brush through her tangled hair, she wondered what it was about men that made them so thoughtless, so selfish, so idiotic.

Well, whatever it was, she was through playing these games. She did not care what her mother or Gisela said, men were worse than the scum on her boots!

9

The shopkeeper added another silk sari to the growing pile in front of Cassandra. She had asked to go sari shopping with Gisela earlier in the week, but now just had no heart for it.

There was no point in buying beautiful saris since she never wanted to go into society again.

"Oh, Cassandra, this is one that you must take, my dear! Why, it is beautiful. Just feel the silk! It's lovely."

Gisela was trying to entice her, just as she had with all of the other saris the shopkeeper had put out for her inspection.

The fabric in front of her was indeed very soft and lovely to touch, but the pale pink color did not excite her. None of the saris did, nor did anything else.

Gisela had taken the lead with the shopkeeper, as he sat cross-legged on his spotlessly white divan, his wares arrayed enticingly in a riot of exotic colors and textures. Cassandra had just sat on the little velvet chair the man had provided, sadly looking at the saris spread before her and stacked in cloth-wrapped bundles behind him.

Asking for softly colored, plain saris, Gisela had tried to bring Cassandra out of the sullens that had settled into her overnight. But it was not working. Cassandra still could not bring herself to find anything interesting today.

"If you would give us a few moments to decide which ones she will take," Gisela said to the shopkeeper. He gave a small bow and then left to see to the folding of another customer's rejected saris.

"What is it, Cassandra? You have been shown so many lovely saris and have hardly even looked at one. What is wrong, my dear?"

Cassandra wiped away a tear that threatened to fall on to the delicate fabric in front of her.

"Major Vernon. I overheard him speaking to some men last night. He . . . he spoke of me as if I was some prize to be won. He even said that he did not care what I looked like. My father would get him a good job in the government and I had a nice sized dowry, and that was all that mattered."

Cassandra could not hold back her tears any longer. "He . . . he even said that he, he hated my, my giggle."

She felt around in her reticule for her handkerchief, but as usual, she had forgotten to put one in.

A little hand came forward with a large white handkerchief in it. Sweet little Harry, who had accompanied her on her shopping trip, had come prepared. His little brow was furrowed with worry as he stood by her.

"Miss, do not cry," he pleaded.

"No, really Cassandra, Major Vernon is not worth even one of your tears," Gisela said, patting her arm consolingly.

"He—he is just like Fel—Felbridge. Oh, Gisela, all men *are* the same!" Cassandra blew her nose and tried to stop crying.

"No, they most certainly are not! Why, has Mr. Ritchie ever done anything to make you think that he is of the same stamp as Lord Felbridge?"

Cassandra sniffed into her handkerchief. "No."

"No, indeed he has not. And he would not. He is an upstanding young man."

Cassandra looked back at the pale colored silks in front of her. They were indeed beautiful, but they were not right. Major Vernon was not right for her either, but nothing she could have said to her mother would have stopped her from pushing him at her.

"Anyway, I'm not entirely sure why you are so upset over what Major Vernon had to say. You did not harbor any feelings for him, did you?"

"No," Cassandra said, wiping away her tears.

"No, I thought not," Gisela gave Cassandra a sly smile and then turned back to the saris.

"It is just that his actions have confirmed what I thought all along about men, Gisela." Cassandra idly fingered the soft silk.

"But it is not true, my dear. It is unfortunate that there are men like Lord Felbridge and Major Vernon, but not *all* men are like that. I certainly do not put Mr. Brown in that category."

"You truly believe that Mr. Ritchie is different?" Cassandra was still not convinced.

"Yes, I do," Gisela said emphatically.

Was it true, was he different? At least he was not overly concerned with fashion and society, as was Lord Felbridge. And he already had a position with her father, so he could not want that from her, as Major Vernon did. Could he truly not have any ulterior motive for wanting to be with her?

Cassandra thought about it for a moment, shifting through the pale-colored saris and dabbing at her eyes with her handkerchief.

A stack of saris behind the shopkeeper attracted her attention. They were brilliantly colored, the gold heavily embroidered on them shimmering in the sunlight.

One in particular caught her eye. It was turquoise, the exact color of Mr. Ritchie's eyes. It was different, so very different, from the other insipid saris in front of her.

Cassandra dried her eyes and motioned for the shopkeeper to come over to attend to them. Uncovering one pale blue silk with silver embroidered along the edges from the pile in front of her, she said, "I will take this one, but I want to see something brighter as well. These colors are too bland. May I see those?" She pointed to the ones behind him.

The shopkeeper set aside the one she had chosen and pushed aside the rest for his assistants to refold. He then set out the stack she had pointed to. The colors reminded Cassandra of the brilliant gemstones found in the jeweler's shop.

Yes, this was what she wanted. She turned to Gisela. "You are certain that all men are not the same? It is so hard to believe, Gisela."

"It may be for you, because you have had two very unfortunate experiences. Believe me, Cassandra, I know. From all that you have told me, Mr. Ritchie sounds like a good man."

Cassandra looked through the saris the man had unfolded and spread before them. She motioned for him to show her the turquoise one.

"He offered to take me to an ancient Hindu temple. It is about two hours' ride from here," Cassandra said, watching the luscious fabric unfold before her eyes. The man let the silk gently glide with a whisper onto her lap, where it lay glittering in the bright sunshine.

It was truly magnificent.

Gisela sucked in her breath,

"It is beautiful, isn't it, Gisela?" She turned to her friend, thinking that she too was in raptures over the sari.

But she was staring wide-eyed at Cassandra herself.

"He offered to take you to a temple? How fascinating! How I envy you, Cassandra! I would love to have an opportunity to learn more about India and its history."

Cassandra contemplated the sari for a moment, while the man unfolded more from the same stack for her inspection.

"Well, then, why don't you come? I was thinking that there would be no way for me to go. Certainly, my mother could never be fobbed off by another shopping story for an all-day outing. But if you come along as a chaperone, Gisela, then we can tell her honestly where we are going."

"But then wouldn't she want to come along as well? And then we shall have a large party and Mr. Ritchie would not be able to act as our tour guide. You are so very lucky, Cassandra, to have such a knowledgeable young man willing to take you around Calcutta."

Gisela sadly fingered the silk sari in front of them. "Mr. Brown has not offered once to show me the sights of Calcutta, as I had hoped he would. He is very busy with his work. I hardly see him at all."

Cassandra placed her hand over her friend's. "I am sorry, Gisela."

"Do you have anything not quite so magnificent?" Gisela asked the man.

He took out another stack of brightly colored saris, but without the gold work all over them. Cassandra picked out a deep pink one, while Gisela pointed to another in pale yellow, both with gold only on the border.

"I assure you, Gisela, even if we were to tell my mother where we were going, she would have no interest in joining us. She does not care to learn more about Calcutta, or indeed, anything Indian," Cassandra said, trying to decide which sari she liked better.

Gisela's face perked up. "Well, in that case, we will certainly have to take advantage of Mr. Ritchie's very kind offer, won't we?"

Cassandra smiled, beginning to feel happy again, for indeed, she could not stay upset for long.

"Yes, and I will take this sari, the turquoise sari and one more in a different design," she said, putting the pink sari on top of the pale blue one she had already chosen.

Friday could not have approached any slower. Cassandra was still not entirely convinced by Gisela's assurances that Mr. Ritchie was different from other men.

All the gentlemen she met seemed as unconcerned with her, her thoughts, or her ideas as Major Vernon. They only gave meaningless compliments to her and talked about themselves.

It was with much trepidation that she dressed for her outing with Mr. Ritchie. Knowing that it was going to be warm, she chose a thin white cotton gown with sunny yellow flowers all over it.

She hoped the dress would make her feel as happy as it looked.

A yellow ribbon was tied around the high waistline just below her bosom, and a matching ribbon was attached to her bonnet to tie into a pretty bow, rakishly set off to the side.

The color of the ribbon gave a pretty pink glow to her cheeks. That was a good omen, she thought, as she checked her reflection in the mirror. Surely if one looked happy, one would be happy.

Both Cassandra and Gisela found the drive to the temple to be fascinating.

It was very easy to tell exactly at which point they left the city. There were no houses just outside of the city, only farmland of varying shades of green.

Gisela pointed out the different crops, asking Mr. Ritchie to identify them. The only one he could positively point out was the rice, which was the lightest green in color and standing in pools of water. He was, however, able to give them some of the history of the area and a few amusing anecdotes of English-Indian miscommunication.

The road itself was no more than a wide path built up between waterways. Every so often, there was open water where women could be seen washing clothes or rinsing out cooking utensils.

Close to these open spots, there were generally some thatched huts, with woven mats for the walls similar to the poorer homes in Calcutta. Julian called them villages, although the ladies thought that was being very generous.

Trees lined the road, separating it from the waterways. They also provided a lovely shady canopy under which to drive. The drive was pleasant and the road empty, save for a few farmers pulling bullock carts loaded with vegetables or wood.

After nearly two hours, the trees began to grow thicker and the water less frequent, and before they knew it they were in the midst of a jungle.

A fork in the road stopped them, and Cassandra looked to Mr. Ritchie questioningly. He just smiled and said that one way led to the temple and the other to the guesthouse. As it was nearing midday, he suggested that they go to the temple for their picnic.

"Picnic? But we have not brought a picnic!" Cassandra looked behind the bench for a picnic basket, but there was none. She had expected that they would take tiffin, the Indian word for lunch, at the guesthouse.

There was such a mischievous twinkle in Mr. Ritchie's bright turquoise eyes that Cassandra had to laugh. Saying nothing, he directed his horse down the smaller of the two lanes.

After such a lovely drive with pleasant conversation, Mr. Ritchie had not only completely set Cassandra at her ease, but was also a charming companion and tour guide. And she was very pleased to note that he had paid as much attention to Gisela as he had to her.

And not one flowery compliment had passed his lips!

Cassandra was very happy with the day, and beginning to think that Gisela had been right—Mr. Ritchie *was* different than other men.

When they arrived at the temple site, they found that there was quite a substantial picnic laid out for them. Mr. Ritchie had cleverly sent his servants out earlier that morning, so that they could set up everything before they arrived.

A table and three chairs were placed under the canopy of a nearby banyan tree.

Although they had not seen the temple yet, Mr.

Ritchie told them that they were close enough to it that they could easily walk to view the structure. But they were not so close that anyone else who might have come to see the temple would disturb them.

The shade of the tree was very cooling, and the iced lemonade made Cassandra feel as if she were in heaven after their long and hot drive.

As they finished their meal, Mr. Ritchie cleared his throat awkwardly. "Shall we walk to the temple now?" he suggested.

Cassandra looked eagerly at Gisela. At her smiling agreement, they began to pick their way carefully through the overgrown path that led to the structure.

"The temple dates from ancient times, and was probably built over five hundred years ago," Mr. Ritchie explained. "The kings who ruled this region at the time were worshippers of the god Shiva, the major male god in the Hindu pantheon."

They had emerged from the shaded path into a bright clearing in the jungle. Cassandra's eyes, dazzled by the sunlight, just began to register the beautiful proportions of the building before them.

"They built the temple both as a tribute to him and as their legacy for the ages," Mr. Ritchie continued. "Over the centuries, it has fallen into disuse and is no longer an active place of worship. Today, it is simply a place to be visited by sightseers like us—more for its spectacular artwork than for its religious significance."

The temple was smaller than she had imagined—certainly not as grand as the cathedrals back home. It was a square structure that was perhaps thirty feet high, and topped by an elegant spire that rose to just above the tops of the surrounding trees.

As they drew closer, she heard Gisela gasp. It was then that her eyes were drawn to the artwork that decorated the walls of the temple.

Every inch of each of the wall facing them was covered with marvelously detailed sculptures of people, row upon row, rising up to the top of the spire. Naked men and women, with no anatomical detail left to the imagination. Beautiful women in sinuous positions, with pinched waists, perfectly rounded breasts and flared hips.

And the men . . . Cassandra's cheeks were aflame.

Stealing looks from under her eyelashes as they slowly approached the temple, Cassandra's gaze was arrested by the sculpture of a man at the center of a frieze. He was startlingly handsome, with the fine musculature in his arms and chest lovingly detailed by the ancient, anonymous sculptor.

And then her eyes swept down his body. . . .

In her eighteen years, Cassandra had never seen a naked man, although she had some basic knowledge of a man's form. The reality and detail of the sculptures, however, were overwhelming.

It was then that Cassandra completely lost any good humor that she had harbored that day. Gisela had been wrong—Mr. Ritchie was *exactly* like all other men. Why else would he bring her to see this?

Her quick temper flared and she turned to Mr. Ritchie to give him the dressing down of his life.

Gisela was too quick for her, however. Before Cassandra could even open her mouth to give him one of the scathing remarks that had immediately sprung to her mind, she was abruptly and a little violently pulled away.

"Cassandra, may I speak to you for a moment?" she said as she dragged Cassandra off toward the path.

"Do not say a word!" she said, as soon as they were out of earshot of Mr. Ritchie.

"Gisela!"

"Not one word."

Cassandra ground her teeth together, but kept her mouth shut.

"Now I know what you are thinking, and you are wrong. I do not believe that Mr. Ritchie has any ulterior motives in bringing you here. If he did, he certainly would not have brought me as well. Would he?"

Cassandra did not say anything, but it was difficult to hear what Gisela was saying for the pounding anger ringing in her ears.

"I am certain that there is a very reasonable explanation for this, and I am willing to hear it from Mr. Ritchie." She paused and looked sternly at Cassandra. "And so will you."

"Gisela, I do not honestly know if I can stand there and listen with any equanimity to whatever excuse he is going to make up," Cassandra said hotly.

"You must. Remember, you are the one who told him that you wanted to learn more about Indian culture. Well, he is showing it to you. You cannot now turn your back on him and his culture just because it offends your delicate English sensibilities."

Cassandra took a deep breath to calm her anger. Gisela was right. Surely he had a reasonable explanation for bringing them here.

Cassandra nodded. "All right, Gisela. Let us hear what Mr. Ritchie has to say."

They walked back to him. He was standing by the side of the temple, looking very upset.

He approached them as they walked toward him. "Miss Renwick, Mrs. Brown, please accept my most profuse apologies. I did not mean to shock you, or upset you with this."

"No need, Mr. Ritchie," Gisela said. "We would like to learn more about the temple and the sculptures that adorn it."

"You are very forgiving. I appreciate that." He paused, carefully choosing his words. "The art that you see here is somewhat unusual, even in Indian art, although the style of the figures is not. The ancient Indians were very free about . . ."

He paused once again, then took a deep breath and plunged on, ". . . about love and the relationship between men and women."

Cassandra watched Mr. Ritchie as he gave what

seemed to be a well-practiced speech. Had he thought about this before he brought them here? *Had* he done this on purpose? Or had he practiced his speech in anticipation of teaching them something new and interesting? Cassandra just could not make up her mind.

"The people of those times felt that the joy of the . . . the intimate relationship between men and women was so special, so elevating, that it was one of the many approximations of the joy that one felt in communing with God," he continued.

"They felt no shame in displaying the beauty of the human body—after all, to them, the beauty of the gods is revealed through the human form created by the gods in their own image."

"So what we are seeing here is a form of worship?"

"Yes, precisely! The depictions show people worshiping Shiva even as they worship and have, er, relations with each other."

He paused and looked back at the temple and then down to the ground in front of them. "It was, however, entirely inappropriate for me to bring you here. I sincerely hope that I have not offended you by doing so. There are so many other things, innocent and interesting things, that I could show you—like the Kali Temple just south of Calcutta—although that you might find rather gruesome. Kali is a goddess who wears a necklace of human skulls."

Cassandra felt her heart soften at Mr. Ritchie's dilemma as he stood looking both confused and chagrined. "I have to admit to preferring this to something bloody and gruesome," she admitted.

He perked up a little at this and even managed a little smile, but Gisela said, "I am not entirely sure that I agree. However, I believe it is time that we went to the guesthouse, if that is all right, Mr. Ritchie?"

"Oh yes, of course! Please excuse my thoughtlessness. You must be very tired after the long journey." He led the way back into the jungle and to his phaeton.

Cassandra wanted to believe Mr. Ritchie had planned this trip in all innocence. *He is different from other men*, she told herself again.

The thought that she was not interested in men came back into her mind. But somehow, she just didn't seem to have the same strength of conviction anymore.

10

"Miss Renwick, I must apologize again. I am rather ashamed, actually, to have brought you to see this temple. It was . . . well, inappropriate."

"Oh no, Mr. Ritchie, think no more about it."

Julian was sitting with Miss Renwick on a bench in the shade of a tree behind the guesthouse. The garden around them was filled with large colorful flowers, artistically arranged into formal beds.

Julian had been rather loath to break the gentle silence that surrounded them. But he still felt uncertain about the wisdom of this outing. It was true that he was trying to make her fall in love with him, but he would never do anything to hurt her.

Miss Renwick suddenly began to giggle. It was soft at first, but then it grew until her shoulders were shaking with it.

Julian could not imagine what she had found so amusing in this garden, or, in fact, any of the events of the day so far.

He turned to ask her, when she said, "I am sorry, I was just thinking how ridiculous I have been."

"Ridiculous? How?"

"Just my reaction to the sculptures on the temple walls. I was so embarrassed by . . ."—she searched for a modest

way of saying it—". . . by the realism in the human forms
that I failed to even look at the sculptures in their entirety
or indeed at the temple itself. It really was quite wrong and
very silly of me, I am afraid."

"Oh no, I completely understand your reluctance to
truly look at it. Indeed, it was not silly at all—as I said, I
should not have brought you here. It was most inappropriate of me, but I had forgotten how explicit the sculptures are. I have not been here in a very long time."

He continued softly, "I do hope you will accept my
apologies, Miss Renwick."

"But it is I who owe you one for not appreciating the
art, which is clearly an important part of the culture. I
asked to learn more about India, and you have held up
your end of the bargain. But I have not."

Miss Renwick's eyes suddenly opened wider and she
turned her open face toward Julian once again. "But perhaps it is not too late! Do you think we could go back to
the temple so that I may truly look at it again?"

Julian thought of her first reaction to the temple and
his own when he saw it while standing beside her. The
heat that had suddenly suffused him. No, going back to
the temple would *not* be a good idea.

"I am sorry, Miss Renwick . . ."

"Oh, please?"

"But Mrs. Brown is still resting."

"Yes, that is why just now would be a perfect time to go.
Wouldn't it be a nice way to pass the time while she rests?"

"It is really not proper . . ." he began.

Miss Renwick stood up, looking at him beseechingly.
She gave him the sweetest, most pleading expression. He
nearly laughed at how adorable she looked.

"Very well, but we will have to hurry, so that we can
return with no one the wiser," he finally relented.

Immediately upon reaching the site of the temple,
Julian knew for certain that it had been a mistake.

Despite the fact that she had just seen it only one hour
earlier, Miss Renwick's face had a look of amazement as

they came closer to the intricate carvings which decorated the outside of the temple. Her cheeks, once again,
flamed with embarrassment.

But this time, she was clearly determined to actually
look carefully at the sculptures, instead of turning away
in shame as she had done before.

Julian, on the other hand, found that his mind and
body were in a riot of desire, conflicting with the re-
straint he knew was demanded. His palms were sweating
as he fought to control his wayward thoughts.

It would have been so much easier if Mrs. Brown had
been with them. Her presence would have cooled his
ardor with no problem.

But now, there was nothing, no distractions.

Only Miss Renwick's determined face, her sweet lips,
her lovely figure . . . Julian abruptly pulled his mind
away. Control was the watchword of the day.

As they circled the temple looking at the intricate
carvings, the wind began to pick up. And without further
warning, they were suddenly deluged with rain.

Miss Renwick stopped in her tracks and looked to Julian
with surprise and chagrin, as if asking him to stop the
storm.

Julian, too, was completely taken by surprise by the
sudden squall, but he reacted quickly. Grabbing Miss
Renwick's hand, he ran with her to the banyan tree
where they had had their luncheon. All traces of their
picnic were now gone.

The wide, lush growth of leaves and branches of the
tree formed a natural shelter from the rain. The
branches reached out and then gracefully dropped
down to the ground to form leafy pillars, which pro-
tected them from the tempest.

Panting slightly from their run, they stood under the
shelter of the tree, staring out at the storm. Miss Renwick
was shivering in her thin white dress, which had become
completely transparent now that it was wet.

Julian swallowed hard, willing his body not to react.

He needed to behave himself. He removed his coat and wrapped it gently around Cassandra's shoulders, hoping that if he didn't see her, it would be easier to control himself.

Large blue eyes looked gratefully up at him—and he was lost.

Much as she tried, Cassandra could not keep her eyes from roving over the fine white cotton of Julian's shirt. His brown, muscled arms showed clearly through the thin, damp material. If it were not for his waistcoat, she imagined that there would be much more of Julian's body exposed for her pleasure—much like the powerful torsos of the sculpted men on the temple walls.

She shivered, although this time it was not due to the cold. Her eyes moved slowly up from his chest, over his now-wilted neckcloth, to his face. His deep pink lips looked incredibly enticing, but she did not stop there. She let her gaze drift upward to look into his eyes, which now were deep pools of turquoise.

The unmasked passion revealed there made Cassandra feel as if a flow of hot lava was running down into the pit of her stomach. The heat slid further down her body.

Cassandra could not move. Slowly, he reached for her, ever so gently cradling her face in his large, warm brown hands. He kissed her, gently at first and then with an ever-growing passion.

She felt as if he were completely encompassing her, and it felt so good!

A tremor of delight coursed through her body. She moved ever so slightly, but just enough to mold her body to his. The sensations as she felt his hard body against her own almost caused her to swoon.

He gently teased her tongue, intertwining his own with hers when she opened her mouth to him. Then his hands slowly moved down from her face to her shoulders.

Cassandra gasped at the fire that had begun burning

within her—a fire that grew more insistent as Julian's mouth moved from hers, slowly making its way down her neck and then continuing down to the pounding at the base of her throat.

His hands moved farther down her body as well, following her curves until they rested, one at her waist, the other on her breast. His thumb moved gently over her nipple. She arched her back, wanting more, knowing that he was prepared to give it.

His lips had just closed around her sensitive flesh when she heard a faint voice calling out her name. The last drips of rain plopped loudly on to the leaves around them.

The voice called again, this time coming closer.

Julian looked up, and Cassandra jumped away from him as if he had suddenly turned into a raging fire. Their eyes locked in shocked surprise.

Someone was looking for them!

In a shaky voice, Cassandra called out a response. She adjusted her dress and then wrapped Julian's jacket around herself so that she was as decently covered as possible in her soaking wet dress.

Julian had turned his back to her to lean with one hand against the trunk of the tree. She could hear him taking a few deep cooling breaths of air.

Gisela came around a bend in the path. She was holding a black umbrella and looking very worried. Sudden relief flooded her face as she approached the tree.

"Oh, thank God you are safe!"

"Why, of course we are safe, Gisela," Cassandra forced a little laugh. "As you can see, we only suffer from a thorough wetting."

"I was so worried when I woke up at the sound of the storm and then found you both gone! I borrowed a cart and forced the innkeeper to bring me here to look for you!" It was clear that Gisela was still upset.

Cassandra ran and put her arms around her dear friend. "Oh, I am so sorry, Gisela. We did not mean to alarm you. In fact, we were hoping to return before you awoke, but the storm caught us by surprise."

Gisela looked down at Cassandra wrapped in Julian's coat. "So I see."

Cassandra self-consciously drew it tighter.

"Let us return to the guesthouse and see if they can do anything to dry your dress quickly and give you something more decent to wear."

"Oh, yes, do let us. I am afraid I am not very comfortable this way," Cassandra said, happy to pull Gisela's attention away from Julian and what she had been doing there with him.

While Cassandra's dress was being ironed dry, she borrowed a light wrapper from the innkeeper's wife. Clutching a shawl around her, Cassandra sat with Gisela in the upstairs bedroom.

Gisela took a deep breath. "Cassandra. . . ."

"Yes?" Cassandra replied nervously.

"What made you go back to the temple alone with Mr. Ritchie? Did you not realize that that was a highly improper thing to do?"

Cassandra looked down at her hands, suddenly ashamed at her boldness. What had, only a short time ago, seemed like a wonderful idea now seemed very wrong indeed.

"I am sorry, Gisela. I . . . I did not stop to think about that."

"You are so young, my dear." Gisela shook her head sadly. "And so inexperienced in the ways of the world. Indeed, I do not know what they taught you at that school you attended."

Cassandra sat in silence. She *had* learned not to go off alone with men, but in her excitement, she had forgotten, or deliberately ignored, what she had learned.

Gisela went on firmly. "I suppose your mother assumed, as did I, that you had learned proper rules of behavior."

"I have! I . . . I just did not follow them." Cassandra felt close to tears. This quiet rebuke from her friend touched her much more deeply than any of her mother's loud scolds about her lack of proper decorum.

Gisela sighed audibly, but stopped suddenly and asked, "Cassandra, did Mr. Ritchie . . ." she paused for the right words. "Did Mr. Ritchie behave improperly toward you while you were waiting for the rain to stop?"

Cassandra's tear-filled eyes flew up to Gisela. "No!" she said, a little too quickly and vehemently.

Then, hearing the shrillness in her voice, she moderated her tone. "No, he behaved with all the propriety in the world."

"I did not mean to imply anything, Cassandra. It was just such a suggestive atmosphere. But I know that Mr. Ritchie is a very correct young man who is fully aware of society's rules even if you are not."

Then Gisela smiled and put her hand on her friend's shoulder. "I am happy to hear that nothing happened. For if anything had, I would have been responsible. As it is, I am very grateful for Mr. Ritchie's obvious self-restraint, as, I am sure, are you."

Gisela paused to gather her thoughts. "I need not remind you, Cassandra, not to say anything about this to your mother, or indeed, to anybody. If your parents or anybody in society found out . . . well, let us just say that it would not be good."

Cassandra wondered at Gisela's lightly veiled message. She had heard of one girl who had been alone with a young man and was then forced to marry him. Surely such a thing would not happen to her and Julian? Still, it was better to be careful and to follow Gisela's advice.

"No, Gisela. I do not believe that this entire outing need be mentioned to anyone."

She then gave Gisela her best attempt at a smile. Gisela said no more, but reached out to warmly clasp her friend's hand, just as the maid appeared with Cassandra's dress.

* * *

At the same time that Gisela was thinking he was a complete gentleman, Julian, waiting in a private parlor on the ground floor, was kicking himself for his obvious lack of self-control.

How could he have taken such advantage of the situation?

He dearly hoped that he had not destroyed his rapport with Cassandra. She had every right to be furious with him. She had every right not to speak to him ever again.

And then all of his plans would be at an end. Of course he would deserve whatever it was he had coming to him. He had behaved like a cad.

He wondered just how much she would tell Mrs. Brown. Surely she would say something to her about what had happened between them.

But as the two ladies entered the room, he was surprised to see that they were both smiling with obvious good will toward each other and him. He forced a smile to his own lips and pushed his thoughts and worries to the back of his mind until he could find out what Cassandra had told her chaperone.

"Shall we partake of some tea before we attempt the long drive back?" he offered, in as lighthearted a voice as he could muster.

"That sounds wonderful," Mrs. Brown responded, likewise, with slightly forced cheer.

Julian was eager to get Cassandra alone to ask if she had told Mrs. Brown anything. But after their previous lapse, it was certain that Mrs. Brown was not going to let Cassandra out of her sight for a moment.

Cassandra gave Julian a shy, sweet smile, however, calming his fears. If she could look at him like that, then perhaps there was hope. Could it be that she had not said anything?

A servant came in bearing the tea tray. It was filled

with traditional English tea sandwiches and pastries, as well as a wonderful assortment of Bengali sweets.

The three of them, in pleasant companionship, emptied the plates of all the treats, talking of inconsequential things until it was time to go.

Julian could not wait. He could not sit idly by waiting for Cassandra to seek him out in her father's library.

He had to do something. But what? And where?

He needed to find out what she had said to Mrs. Brown and how she felt about him. Would she still see him or was she angry with him for taking liberties? Not knowing how she felt was the worst sort of torture any man could be in, but it was especially hard for him.

Julian knew his case was special. He didn't know if he was going to be dragged away to prison at any moment for touching a white woman or whether he would be forced to marry her. Either one was a distinct possibility, depending on whether he was considered English or Indian.

And this time he did not believe that his father's influence would be able to help him, as it had when he had graduated from school and was trying to get a job.

Julian paced back and forth. He could not get any work done. He had not been able to focus his mind on anything in the two days since he had come back from the temple.

Although she had tried to pry it out of him, his mother could not figure out what was wrong with him. But how could he possibly tell her?

Nor could he talk to Reggie, his best friend. There was only so far you could trust a friend and Julian wasn't willing to go that far.

No, he was all alone. Alone with his fears and his worries. His concerns were real and they ate at him like a cancer. If only he knew how she felt and what she had done.

He had to do something.

He pulled out a blank piece of paper from Sir Lionel's desk and scribbled a hasty note on it. He pulled the bell for a servant.

Little Harry answered his summons.

He smiled at the self-important little man. In a very short time, Harry had made himself irreplaceable. The entire family, but especially Cassandra, now relied on this boy to carry out so many of their everyday little jobs. And now it was Julian's turn.

He handed the note to the boy. "Take this to Miss Cassandra, Harry. Be sure she gets it in her hand and return to me with her answer."

Harry salaamed and then, taking the note, ran off on his errand.

Julian returned to his desk and put his head in his hands. The response to that note could decide whether he was a free man or a prisoner.

And, even more importantly, how the angelic young woman, who dominated his every thought, felt about him.

11

Cassandra waited by the river dock, her horse shifting restlessly under her. Julian had said in his note to meet him here, but now he was late.

He had never been late before.

She was not certain that she liked this area of Calcutta. It was unusually quiet, or perhaps it was just the time of day. Even her groom's presence nearby did not soothe her nerves.

The sun was just beginning to set, even though it was just after six. She supposed everyone had gone home to their evening meal. Even the usual foot traffic along the streets was lighter, with only a few coolies out running errands for their employers.

"Forgive me, Miss Renwick." Julian's smooth baritone startled her. He was standing right next to her horse, holding its bridle. How had she not seen him approach?

"Oh! Mr. Ritchie, I did not hear you," Cassandra said, putting her hand to her heart, which was pounding in her chest.

"I am sorry, I was negotiating with a boatman and it took longer than I expected."

He helped Cassandra down from her horse and tied it to a nearby tree.

"Are we going for a ride on the river?"

"Yes, I hope that that is all right?"

"Oh, yes! I have not seen Calcutta from the river since the day I arrived. It should be fascinating now that I know more about the city."

Julian smiled. "I hope you will find it so."

He led her to a small one-sailed boat. It was one of many other boats exactly like it on the river.

Taking the oar, Julian paddled through the quieting evening, using the sail to help him fight against the strong current of the river.

As she watched, the sky faded from blue to violet to indigo, with millions of stars appearing overhead and a three-quarter moon lighting their way. She wondered if she would ever get used to the speed of the Indian sunset—in little more than a breath it moved from day to evening to night.

The soft sounds of women's voices as they bathed and washed their clothing along the banks faded as Julian maneuvered the boat to the center of the river and then farther upstream. The gently lapping water and the sound of the sail flipping in the light breeze filled in the silence.

The breeze, which ruffled Cassandra's gown, still carried the heat of the day. She did not feel the need for her shawl, but only enjoyed the soft caress of the air.

There were very few boats out now and certainly none this far out. Cassandra wondered what Julian had planned for her out here in the middle of the river.

It was wonderful to be alone with Julian again. Her Julian.

Things had changed immeasurably between them after their brief interlude at the temple. And now the two of them were alone again—illicitly, wonderfully alone. She felt her heart fluttering like the sail and wondered if he would kiss her.

She realized now that there was no question about her feelings for him. She loved him.

It felt good to finally admit it to herself and, in her own way, to him. Willing her love for him to shine through her eyes, she reached out and took his hand. He looked at her but knew, as she did, that words were unnecessary.

Putting the oar up and setting the sail so that they would float gently back downriver on the current, he looked deeply into her eyes.

He was worried at first, Cassandra could see that. But then, as her love shone through to him, he relaxed.

She didn't need to say anything, he just knew.

Taking her hands in both of his, he softly caressed the back of her hands with his long fingers and then lovingly kissed each finger in turn. Chills shot up her arm and she stifled the urge to giggle. What a wonderful feeling it was to be loved!

A nagging worry tugged at the back of her mind. How could they be together? What would her parents say when they found out? Would they cut her off? Not give him her dowry?

Cassandra firmly pushed the nasty thoughts to the back of her mind. She would not let such things bother her now. For right now, at this time, she would think of nothing other than how much she loved this sweet, thoughtful and wonderful man and how much he loved her in return.

Like her, he did not need to say anything. She could see it in his velvety blue eyes. Eyes that were so filled with passion that just looking into them filled her with the same heat she had felt when he had kissed her under the banyan tree. The heat was so intense that she almost pulled away, but another part of her longed for his sweet kisses once more.

Cassandra did not know how long they sat like that, just gazing into each other's eyes, holding each other's hands. But too soon the women's voices grew louder again. Julian was forced to pay attention once more to the sail, in order to steer them safely back to the dock where the boatman was waiting for them.

In silence, they walked back to where her horse stood waiting for her. She turned to say something to him, but he put his finger to her lips. And then he put his own lips to hers in the lightest of kisses that shot chills down her spine and weakened her knees.

He lifted her into the saddle and then ever so softly whispered, "Good night, Cassandra."

Her groom was waiting for her a discreet distance away. She said nothing but gave Julian her secret loving smile, which he returned.

Julian could not sleep that night. He wandered through the silent house and then up onto the flat roof. He had always come up here when he needed to think or when he was upset.

A light wind blew through the thin cotton of his pajamas. The cool air felt good on his heated body. He paced under a black sky pinpricked with stars.

What had happened?

He still was not sure he understood it. During the past few days, he had been in such torment—not knowing what Cassandra had done and how she felt.

Now, after hardly speaking two words to her, he knew that he loved her and she loved him.

He was amazed at the expressiveness of her eyes. How they had positively glowed with love for him! The sweet, gentle touch of her hand on his—it conveyed so much more than words could ever have said! Yes, there had been a flash of worry, but it was quickly banished in her love for him.

Julian sank to the ground, resting his head against the cool wrought iron railing that surrounded the top of the roof.

He loved her, and he did not know what he was going to do about it.

A warm hand on his shoulder startled him. His mother had come up from behind him without a sound.

"Julian, what is wrong, my son?" she asked, her voice

soothing and musical as the soft sounds of the Bengali words flowed from her.

Julian had the overwhelming desire to curl up in his mother's lap and wish the world away. To rest his head on her soft bosom as he had done when he was a boy and let her smooth the worries from his face and back with her strong hands and soft words.

But he could not do that now. He was a man and he had made a man's decision, and now he had to live with the outcome of it. He had to do what a man should do.

Julian rested his heated forehead against his mother's shoulder for just a moment, gathering the strength to tell her.

He lifted his head. Squaring his shoulders, he said, "Ma, I am going to ask for Cassandra Renwick's hand in marriage."

His mother moved away from him. It was not far, but to Julian it could have been a mile.

"Julian . . ." His mother's voice was full of worry and warning.

"I know you do not approve, but it is something I have to do," he said.

"Why? Why do you have to do this stupid, foolhardy act?"

"Because I love her. And she loves me."

Silence. His mother looked at the trees that surrounded their house, some of them reaching up and over the roof. She pulled away a long strand of graying hair as it whipped across her face and tucked it back into the bun at the nape of her neck.

"I do not understand how you could have done this— fallen in love with an English girl? Did I not warn you of what would happen if you met her?"

Julian sighed. "You did. But I did not listen. I had a plan in mind, but it did not work out the way I had thought."

"A plan? What was this plan?"

"I had thought to make her fall in love with me and

then spurn her as Lady Renwick has spurned me. I had thought to prove to society that I am as good as any Englishman, but it . . . it did not work out that way."

He leaned back against the railing once more, tilting his head up to the stars, but not really seeing them.

"My plan worked in that she fell in love with me," he continued softly. "But I have fallen in love with her as well. I could never hurt her now."

His mother stood up and away from him. "It was a stupid idea to begin with. If you had told me about it, I could have explained that to you."

"Ma . . ."

"No, Julian. You had thought to prove a point to the English? You *wanted* to behave as stupidly as they do? Why did you want to prove that you are as small-minded as they are? Are you not better than that? Can *you* not think beyond the color of your own skin?"

His mother began to pace back and forth, kicking up her sari in front of her as she walked. He had never seen her so angry before.

"And what did you plan to do, once this girl had fallen in love with you? How were going to show society that you were better than they? By treating her badly? By treating her as you have been treated? And was this going to make you feel better—or was it intended to simply make the English hate you even more than they do already?"

"No! Ma, please, listen to me."

"What?" His mother stopped her pacing and stood in front of him, breathing heavily from her exertions.

Julian was suddenly at a loss for words under his mother's angry gaze.

"I . . . I don't know what I was going to do, precisely."

"Ah, very clever!"

"No, listen. But I do know what I am going to do now."

His mother crossed her arms in front of her and looked up at him, ready and waiting.

Julian swallowed. "I am going to ask Sir Lionel for Cassandra's hand in marriage."

"And you think that he will happily accept *you* as his son?"

Julian froze. "I do not know. Probably, he will not, but I have to try. Ma"—he reached out and took her hand, unwinding her arms from in front of her—"I love her. I will do anything—give up my life, my home, my job . . . *anything* for her."

He looked into her eyes and watched as they filled with tears.

"You will be hurt, my son. You will be hurt, and I wish there was something I could do to stop it. But there is nothing. You are a man, and you have acted just . . . almost like your father."

Hastily, she wiped away the tears that had begun to slip down her cheeks. "He too thought he would give up his life for me, but when the time came and he was asked to return to England . . . he left. Do *not* do this, Julian." Her voice came out as little more than a whisper.

Julian took her in his arms. He held her as she cried. Cried for her husband. Cried for him.

"I am sorry, Ma, but I must."

Cassandra attempted to read, but could not focus her mind on the words in front of her. Her wayward thoughts kept going back to Julian and their very special sail along the Hooghly River the previous day.

It had been the most wonderful evening of her life. The way he had looked at her . . .

"Ah, there you are." Lady Renwick suddenly broke in on Cassandra's thoughts, making her blush furiously. "Are you reading again? My dear Cassandra, it is a good thing Major Vernon had not found you so. Why, he would think you a bluestocking."

"Why should I care what Major Vernon thinks, Mama? He does not own me," Cassandra retorted, stung by her mother's criticism.

"Not yet, but I am trying to change that. Surely it does not take an imbecile to see it."

Cassandra bristled. "But I do not want to be owned by Major Vernon. I do not want to be owned by anyone!"

"But you will. You must be married, and when you are, you will be your husband's property and you must do as he says. Honestly, I do not know what they taught you at that school I sent you to for so many years."

Lady Renwick settled herself on the maroon- and white-striped settee across from Cassandra. "It will be Major Vernon to whom you must look for guidance, Cassandra. That is, if we can bring him up to scratch."

"I do not want to bring him up to scratch." Cassandra closed her book with a snap.

"Nonsense! He is precisely the sort of man you should marry, and if I am not mistaken, he is quite sensible of the fact that you are the proper girl for him."

"But Mama, all he is interested in is my dowry and the job that Papa will be able to get him once we are married. He doesn't care for me!"

Her mother looked confused for a moment. "But of course he cares for your dowry. Why else would your papa have given you such a large one if not to attract a good husband?"

Cassandra was shocked. Not that she hadn't known this, but to have it said straight out so boldly! Did her mother not care for her? For her feelings?

"But what about love? I could not marry a man I did not love!"

"Love will come later, my dear. After you have known him and been married to him for some time, you will grow to love him. Do not let that trifle interfere with our plans."

Cassandra began to feel the burn of her anger and struggled to control it. "Mama, there is nothing you can do or say that will convince me to marry Major Vernon."

"Don't be a fool, Cassandra. Of course you will marry

him—even if it is only because your father and I tell you to."

"Surely you and Papa would not force me into marriage?" Cassandra asked, horrified.

"I do hope it will not come to that, Cassandra. But do not press us."

"But I . . . I could not . . . I will not marry Major Vernon!"

Without another word, Cassandra strode to her room. How could her mother expect her to marry that awful Major Vernon? Especially when she had the love of a wonderful man like Julian.

Of course, her mother did not know that Julian loved her, but she would. Julian would come and ask her father for her hand in marriage. She was sure that he would.

He had to—didn't he?

12

"Please, Miss, stop pulling at your dress. It is supposed to be that low," Gita said with exasperation at Cassandra's constant fiddling with the neckline of her new gown.

"But it is too low. Just look at how much is showing!" Cassandra frowned at her reflection in the mirror, as Gita once more adjusted her dress lower. The blush-colored satin underdress already clung almost indecently to her slender figure. Luckily, the silvery net that flowed so nicely over it made it almost unnoticeable, she hoped. How she wished she could be like Julian and not have a care about what she wore, not have to be so fashionable.

She did reluctantly admit that the overall effect was quite fairylike. And the silver necklace, with a single pearl drop hanging very close to her cleavage so as to draw the eye downward, was too elegant to be changed. It also matched the pearl-drop earrings her mother had lent her to go with it.

No, she resolved, there was nothing that could be done to cover herself more decently, at least not without changing her whole dress, and her mother would not hear of that.

Cassandra sighed and then gave Gita a little smile as the ayah twitched a bit of fabric into a better place.

She wished Julian could be there, but it was extremely

unlikely that he would be invited to this evening's entertainment. It made the whole evening seem rather insipid. If she had had a choice, Cassandra would have much preferred to stay in her room rather than attend a dance without Julian.

She knew why her mother had insisted on her wearing this dress. This was to be the last maneuver in her mother's campaign to get Major Vernon to propose. Cassandra determined to avoid him as much as she could.

The drawing room was as yet empty of guests when Cassandra joined her parents. Her mother gave her a little tight-lipped smile, but still nodded her head approvingly, while Sir Lionel beamed indulgently at his daughter.

"I hope, Cassandra, that you will do your all to put Major Vernon at ease," her mother said pointedly. What was implied was to make Major Vernon's conquest easy, and Cassandra knew it.

"Mother, I believe we discussed this earlier, and I have nothing more to add at this time," Cassandra said very stiffly. Then, as the first of the guests began to arrive, she plastered a smile on to her face.

Sir Lionel, who had had no time to talk with his wife all day, looked questioningly at Lady Renwick. She simply scowled in return, and then too put on her social smile and moved to greet her guests.

Cassandra was not at all surprised that Major Vernon was seated next to her at dinner. He was as charming as he could possibly be, while Cassandra was as cool as possible without being overtly offensive.

"Cassandra, you will behave properly," her mother whispered harshly in her ear as they greeted the guests who were invited to the dance only.

With a sigh, Cassandra allowed her inner actress free rein, for she certainly did not have the heart to smile and be charming to all who approached her. Very quickly, her dances were spoken for, and she was pleased with herself for managing to keep Major Vernon from claiming more than one.

Captain George led her out for the second country dance.

"You are looking very pretty this evening, Miss Renwick," he said soon after they had taken their places on the dance floor.

"Thank you, sir."

"I believe I am quite lucky to have secured a dance with you."

Cassandra forced a laugh. "Indeed, most of my dances were bespoken before the musicians were even finished warming up. I must admit that it is quite thrilling to be so sought after," she lied glibly.

The captain nodded his head, but smiled a rather knowing smile. "Yet, I hear that very soon you may not be available to so many gentlemen."

Cassandra narrowed her eyes, all thoughts of carrying on her pretense gone. "I am sorry, but I do not take your meaning."

The captain's smiled broadened. "Why, I am referring to Major Vernon, of course."

Cassandra pinched together her lips to keep the sharp retort that sprang to her mind from stealing out of her mouth. "You are mistaken, sir; there is nothing between Major Vernon and me."

The captain lost his smile immediately. "I am very sorry if I have offended you. I was only repeating what everyone has been saying."

"Well, then, I would appreciate it if you would correct anyone you hear utter such foolishness."

This was all part of her mother's plan, she was sure. Spreading the rumor that she and Major Vernon were all but betrothed was just like Lady Renwick. But Cassandra would do all that she could to see that this plan failed.

Sighing, she pasted her smile back on her face. It would not do to let everyone see how upset she was. "Do let us talk of more pleasant things, Captain," she said lightly.

The captain was mollified and immediately engaged

her in some light meaningless banter, in which Cassandra joined with aplomb.

Three dances later, Cassandra felt she must get some fresh air. As she had hoped, her next dance partner was more than happy to take her for a stroll through the garden.

They had not gone very far, however, when Major Vernon stepped up to them. "Lieutenant, Miss Scottsdale is looking for you, I believe."

The gentleman turned to Cassandra, while taking a step back toward the house. "You must forgive me, Miss Renwick. . . ."

Cassandra laughed at his eagerness. "Yes, of course, sir. Do not give me one moment's thought."

"I shall carry on, Lieutenant," Major Vernon offered.

"Thank you, sir." The young man bowed to them both and then walked quickly back to the house.

"That was easy," Major Vernon said as he took Cassandra's arm.

"I beg your pardon?"

"Oh, nothing, Miss Renwick, nothing at all."

They continued walking slowly along the path, but Cassandra had a strong feeling that she and the Lieutenant had just been duped.

With a sudden movement, Major Vernon pulled Cassandra off the path and dropped down onto one knee before her.

"Miss Renwick," he began, his voice filled with emotion. "No, Cassandra, if I may call you that, I would be most honored if you would consent to become my wife."

Then, before Cassandra could even open her mouth to deny him, he was back up again crushing her in his embrace and planting a wet kiss upon her lips.

Cassandra nearly screamed, but caught herself just in time. She did not want an audience, of that she was sure. Otherwise she would certainly be trapped into marrying this horrid man.

Cassandra pushed away from Major Vernon. "Do not ever do that again!" she said vehemently.

"But I love you!" he protested.

"Fiddlesticks!"

"I beg your pardon?"

"I said, fiddlesticks. You do not love me; all you are interested in is my dowry and . . ."

"Miss Renwick, no! How could you possibly say such a thing?" Major Vernon feigned shock at her words.

"Coming it on too strong, Major."

"Miss Renwick, whoever told you such lies?"

"No one told me, Major, only yourself. I had the misfortune of overhearing you speaking to some other officers last week at the Mackleys' musicale." Cassandra was thrilled to finally have a chance to call a gentleman on his own words.

Major Vernon opened his mouth in shock, but then, much to Cassandra's surprise, he began laughing.

"And what is so amusing, sir?"

"You surely do not believe that I spoke the truth to those gentlemen? Oh, no, Miss Renwick, I assure you, what you must have overheard was some silly nonsense that I made up. Why, gentlemen do this all the time to hide their true feelings. Otherwise we would become a laughingstock, I assure you."

Cassandra narrowed her eyes. She did not believe one word of this and was about to say so when Major Vernon once more took possession of her hand.

"Please, dear Cassandra, do not let that weigh with you at all. Honestly, I care very deeply for you and I would be honored if you would . . ."

"No," she said, cutting him off.

"I am sorry?"

"I said no. Even if what you say is true, and I do not believe it for one moment, I still could not marry you."

"But, my dear, why?"

"Because, quite simply, Major, I am in love with

Another." There, she had said it. She had told him the truth, and it felt very good.

"Another? And who, may I ask, is that?" the Major asked, taking a step back away from her.

"I am sorry. I am not currently at liberty to say."

"I . . . well, I understand." Major Vernon seemed confused. "Does your mother know of this?"

"No, she does not, and I would appreciate it if you would not say anything to her. I expect this gentleman to declare himself shortly, but until he does, I must ask that you maintain your discretion."

"Yes, yes, of course. I shall escort you back to the house."

"Thank you, but that will not be necessary. If you do not mind, I believe I will stay here a moment to compose myself, alone."

"Of course." Major Vernon slowly and rather dejectedly walked away.

Cassandra took a deep breath and let out a sigh, so glad that that was over with. She need not worry about Major Vernon anymore, that was certain. She felt bad for having to be so honest with him, but there had seemed to be no other way of convincing him of her true feelings.

Before she was entirely aware of it, another gentleman was at her side.

"Excuse me, Miss Renwick."

Cassandra jumped. She had not realized that anyone else was nearby. "Oh, Mr. White!"

"I am sorry to startle you like that. I am afraid I could not help overhearing what you said just now," Mr. White said softly so that only she could hear.

"You did? Oh dear, I do hope that you will respect my wishes and not repeat this . . . this occurrence to my mother—or to my father, for that matter."

"No, of course, I would not do such a thing. But perhaps you will allow me to unburden myself of something that has for some time weighed heavily upon my conscience."

He took a deep breath as if to steady himself to an unwanted task.

"My goodness, Mr. White, this sounds very serious. Whatever could that be? It does not have anything to do with me, I hope."

"I am afraid that it does. And I hold myself completely responsible for not speaking to you about it earlier, perhaps before so much damage was done. But I pray that you will be understanding and not too hurt by what I am about to tell you."

"I am afraid I do not understand you," Cassandra said, as a slow chill began at the bottom of her spine.

"Miss Renwick, I overheard you say to Major Vernon that you were in love with Another. I believe I know who that other is and I beg you to reconsider your feelings."

"You know? How . . . how do you know?"

"I know because I was taken into his confidence when you first asked him to go out riding with you."

"You were? He told you?" Cassandra was quite surprised at his honesty.

"Yes. We are very good friends, you know."

"I see."

"He knew I would never tell anyone about your liaison, and indeed, I have not done so. However, I must tell you one other thing that he told me when he first arranged to see you." He stopped to take another deep breath.

"I am not sure I want to hear this." She did not know what it was, but there was something about Mr. White's demeanor that truly scared her.

"I must . . . I must tell you. And you must know that this is not easy for me. He said that . . . that it would all be a game to make you fall in love with him, no more."

Once Mr. White had started, the words poured out quickly. "Julian feels nothing for you, Miss Renwick. He only did all that he could to make you fall in love with him. He did it so that your mother would be hurt, just as he has been hurt every time she has been rude to him or snubbed him because of his parentage."

As what he said sunk in, the chill sped up Cassandra's spine until, finally, it exploded in her head.

She covered her ears. No, she could not, would not hear what he was saying. It was not true!

He loved her. Julian loved her, she knew it.

Mr. White was lying. He was lying to her because, because . . . she did not know why, but he was, that much she knew.

"Stop! Stop! You are lying. Julian loves me. I know he does!" Cassandra nearly shouted.

Mr. White looked over his shoulder to see if anyone had heard her. "Please, Miss Renwick, lower your voice! I am sorry. I am so sorry. But you must hear the truth. It was a game to Julian, that is all. He feels nothing for you."

Cassandra could not help herself any longer. Hearing the soft, painful note of truth in his voice, she broke down. Her knees buckled from under her and she dropped to the ground, sobbing, crying out her pain.

Mr. White caught her as best he could and lowered her onto the soft grass. He handed her his handkerchief, clearly at a loss of what else to do.

"Please, Miss Renwick, you must not. He is not worthy of you. Do not be so upset."

"He is worthy of me, he is everything to me!" She sobbed harder.

"I am so sorry," he said again. "Can I get your mother for you?"

"No!" Cassandra sat up and tried to stop the tears, but she could not. She managed to hiccup, "Please get Gisela . . . Mrs. Brown."

Cassandra did not remember being brought to her room. She vaguely remembered Promeela coming in and giving her some vile-tasting draft. It had put her to sleep, but did not, unfortunately, last the whole night.

It was still dark when she awoke. There was little she

could do to stop her tears when she remembered the events of the past night.

Was it true? Was it all a game to Julian? But why would Mr. White lie to her?

But he loves me! He said so!

Cassandra thought back to the last time she saw Julian, on the boat. It had been the most special and romantic evening of her life! He had kissed her. He had kissed her even more passionately under the banyan tree by the temple.

But had he ever said the words *I love you*?

No. He had not. He had not said anything.

But then, neither had she, but he had known. He had known that she loved him. They had not needed words, they just knew.

But did she truly know?

That was when the tears started again.

13

It was a very somber and resolute young woman who greeted her parents at the breakfast table later that morning.

"Good morning, Cassandra," her mother said as her daughter entered the breakfast parlor. "I would have a word with you after you are done eating."

"Good morning, Mother, Father," Cassandra replied, turning to each parent in turn. "I would like to have a word with you as well. With both of you, in fact."

Cassandra poured herself a cup of tea. "I would like passage booked on the next ship leaving for England, immediately.

"No, my mind is made up," she said quietly as both her parents looked up at her with surprise. "I cannot stay here, and the only alternative I have is to return to England. I am sure that with a properly worded note concerning the ill-effects the weather here has had on my constitution, Aunt Bradmore will take me in again as she did all through my school years. Perhaps she will even allow me to share in Cousin Olivia's next season—that is, if Olivia has not already found a husband."

Her parents sat stunned for a few moments.

"Cassie, do you truly not wish to marry Major Vernon?

If you don't, you know I would never insist . . ." her father began.

"Cassandra *will* marry Major Vernon, Sir Lionel. Her threats of running away will not alter my decision," her mother said.

Cassandra gave her father a small smile and then turned to face her mother. "No, Mother, I will not marry Major Vernon, as I have told you many times already. But it is not only that which is forcing me to return to England, but . . . but something else of which I would rather not speak." She quickly brushed away the tears welling in her eyes.

"Cassie, there are many more men here in Calcutta if you truly cannot bear to marry Major Vernon," her father said, ignoring her mother for once.

Cassandra said nothing, but just shook her head.

Harry came into the room at that moment with a note on a silver tray, which he proffered to Cassandra. She quickly scanned it, nodded to Harry and then turned to her father.

"I sent Harry with a note to the docks this morning to find when the next ship is leaving for England. There is one sailing this evening, Papa. The captain says that he can accommodate me. And there is a young widow returning to England alone, with whom I will share quarters and who is willing to chaperone me on the journey to London as well."

Both of her parents sat stunned.

"You are not serious!" her mother finally remonstrated. "Cassandra! That is too soon. You cannot leave tonight."

"Yes, I can, Mother. In fact, it is perfect. Excuse me while I go inform Gita. Oh dear, I will miss her so. I have grown very fond of her." Cassandra rushed off without having actually eaten any breakfast.

In her room, Gita packed Cassandra's trunks, dropping in a few unbidden tears along with the clothes. A few kind words from Cassandra was all that was necessary to make her begin to cry outright.

"Oh, Miss. Are you sure that what you are doing is right?" she cried.

"Yes, I am sorry to lose you, Gita, but it is for the best. I cannot stay," Cassandra said. She felt as if a heavy weight sat at the bottom of her stomach.

Gita sniffed, wiping her eyes on the edge of her sari. "What of little Harry, Miss? He will be upset."

Cassandra frowned. She was very sorry to leave little Harry behind, but there was no way that she could take him away from his home. He was just beginning to speak English more fluently and to become fully adjusted to his new life.

"I will be *very* sorry to leave Harry, but there is no other alternative, Gita. I must do this. Please try to understand."

Gita nodded her head and went back to her packing.

Julian rode into the courtyard of the Renwicks' house and jumped down, leaving his horse with a groom. He carried a string of white tuberoses, the same kind he had presented Cassandra with the first time he had met her after her ball. At the door, he asked for her directly.

The butler had not even had time to speak when Lady Renwick emerged from the drawing room.

"Sir Lionel is not here," she said brusquely, frowning at the unwelcome visitor.

"I have not come to see Sir Lionel, Lady Renwick. Well, at least not right away. I am here to see Miss Renwick," Julian answered, ignoring her rudeness.

"She is not here, nor will she be returning. She has left for England. What do you want with her anyway?" she snapped.

Julian ignored her last question. "Left for England? When? Why? No," he paused for a moment, thinking furiously, "I may know why."

Julian looked down at the floor, his eyes only seeing what his heart suddenly felt like, cold marble stone. He turned and slowly walked back to his horse.

She must have realized that there was no way that they could be married and fled in her sorrow.

Julian smiled, even as the tears threatened to spill out of his eyes. She was so wonderful, so thoughtful. She must have known that he was going to give up his life for her and did not want him to do so. That was the only explanation.

But to leave India entirely was a very drastic move. How had she done it so quickly?

Unconsciously, he rode to work. He was still sitting on his horse just outside the Writers' Building wondering about Cassandra, when a voice interrupted his thoughts.

"Julian! What are you doing here? Did you not send a message earlier saying that you were ill?"

Julian looked down at Reggie and gave his friend a sad smile. "Yes, I am."

He slid from his horse. "She has gone, Reggie."

Reggie understood immediately. "It's better this way, Julian."

"No! No, it is not." Julian was suddenly very angry. "She should not have just left like that. I love her!"

Reggie's eyes widened. "Truly? But you said it was just a game! I told her it was just a game."

"You . . . you told her?" Julian found himself shouting. Passers-by stared and moved to the other side of the sidewalk to avoid the altercation.

"It was just a game, Julian. You said so yourself. But she had truly fallen in love with you and turned down a very good marriage proposal thinking that you would do the honorable thing." Reggie looked warily at his friend.

"I *was* going to do the honorable thing, you fool! I was at Clive Street ready to propose to her." Julian felt the blood pounding in his ears.

"I . . . I am sorry, Julian. But it is better this way. You know that, don't you?" Reggie said, nervously.

"No, I do *not* know that." His hands flexed themselves ready to hurt his friend. Friend indeed! "You betrayed me," he growled.

"Yes, I know. I . . . I am sorry, Julian. I truly am. But I had to." Reggie looked at Julian's fists but then boldly looked up again to look Julian straight in the eye.

Julian understood his friend had done what he thought to be right. Before he lost control, he mounted his horse and rode away.

The pounding in his head echoed the horse's hoofbeats as he rode out of town. He had to get away. He rode the animal hard, not caring where he was going.

Finally, hours later, he turned homeward. As he wound his way home, the gray dusk mirrored his emotions. He was slowly dismounting when his mother came running from the house.

"Julian, Julian, where have you been all day? You missed him! He waited and waited, until he could wait no longer. He said he would miss the ship."

Julian looked at his mother numbly. Slowly taking in her distress, but not comprehending her, he said, "What are you talking about, Ma? Who did I miss? What ship?"

"The ship to England. He had to take the ship leaving for England this evening." His mother hung on his sleeve, looking desperately up at him.

"Gone to England this evening? Who was it?" Julian was getting more and more confused.

His mother handed him a letter. "The Englishman said it was all explained in here. But do come inside. It is too late now anyway," she said sadly.

The lines of the letter were closely written and he had a difficult time deciphering them, but in the end he believed he understood it all. He finally looked up at his mother with a sigh.

She sat at the edge of a chair next to him, eagerly waiting for him to finish reading the letter.

"Well?" she asked as he turned back to the first page. "Has your papa finally made good on his promise to send for you? I must say I had completely given up any hope of him doing so. He has had one excuse after another and has completely stopped mentioning it in his letters for the past few years. That he still writes to us and sends money is really all that matters now."

His mother stopped talking abruptly and gripped her hands together.

Julian put the letter down on the table next to him and took hold of his mother's hands. He could hardly bear to look into her worried eyes.

"I am sorry, Ma. Papa has died," he said as gently as he could.

She looked confused. "Your papa has died? But how? How could he be dead? He is so young. . . . No, I suppose he has grown old as I have.

"How . . . how did he die?" she asked again, now blinking away the tears that had begun to slip from her eyes.

"In a carriage accident, it says." Julian picked up the letter again. "But Ma, that is not all."

Julian quickly scanned the lines once again to find what he was looking for. "It says here that Papa was an earl, Ma!"

Julian looked for some recognition of this in his mother's face, but she just grew confused once again.

"An earl? Oh, yes," she said vaguely, "I believe he did mention that once to me. I never paid much attention to it, I was very young and did not understand what it meant. He was an earl?" she asked, still a little confused.

But then her eyes grew very large. "But Julian, that means that you are now an earl!"

"Yes! That is why this man—he must have been Papa's solicitor—wanted me to go to England as soon as possible, to take up Papa's position as the Earl of Huntley! It says here that there is a considerable estate in Kent with earnings of twenty thousand pounds a year!

"Ma, can you imagine? That is why Papa never had any difficulty sending you money every year and sending me to the best schools. He was as rich as Croesus. And now I am to inherit it!"

Julian sat up straighter in his chair, quite in awe of the thought of having such a fortune and a title as well. *My goodness,* he thought, *I even outrank Sir Lionel—he is only a baronet!*

He wondered what Lady Renwick would think of him now that he was an earl. But then, it did not really matter what she thought any more, now that Cassandra was gone.

Cassandra! It suddenly occurred to him that Cassandra was probably on the same ship as the solicitor who had brought him this letter.

Julian unconsciously let out a groan and dropped his head into his hand. He could have been there with her on that ship! There was probably an empty cabin on that same ship which had been reserved for him.

If only he had known. . . . Surely, Sir Lionel would not object to his daughter marrying him now.

Then an idea struck him. He got up and began to pace around the room. He would travel to England, find Cassandra and marry her there!

Life was decidedly looking better.

But then he looked over at his mother, who too was lost in her own thoughts. Tears were running slowly down her cheeks as she silently mourned the loss of her husband.

"I have lost not only a husband, but a son as well," she said sadly, looking up at Julian. She looked down at her hands, and her tears began to flow a little faster as she pulled off the gold bangles that she always wore.

"I won't need these now that I am a widow," she whispered to herself.

Julian fell on his knees in front of her and grasped her trembling hands.

"No, Ma."

She gave him a watery smile and then extracted one of her hands from his. Putting her bracelets into his

hand, she said, "Give them to her. I am sure Miss Renwick will look beautiful in them."

Julian nearly broke down and cried as well. He stead-
ied himself, but said in a choked voice, "I am going to
miss you, Ma."

14

London, April 1811

With a lift of her chin, Cassandra walked into the Debenhams' ball. She was going make a splash. She was going to be hailed as an incomparable tonight, a diamond of the first water. That's what she had decided. That's what she told herself.

She slowed her steps behind her aunt, Lady Bradmore, and allowed her best friend, Olivia, to take the lead. Could she do this? Did she have the ability, the beauty, the charm?

Cassandra straightened her shoulders and moved herself forward again. If she was going to pull it off, she had to do it right, she scolded herself. She could not back down now.

Aunt Bradmore looked at her quizzically before turning to greet their host and hostess. "How do you do, Lord Debenham, Lady Debenham? You remember my daughter, Olivia?" She paused while Olivia made her curtsey. "And my young niece, Cassandra Renwick? Cassandra has recently returned from India."

"Oh my, you poor dear! Whatever made you go to that awful place?" Lady Debenham said, pressing Cassandra's hand.

Cassandra forced a smile onto her face. "It was not awful at all, actually. I found Calcutta fascinating, my lady." *Except, of course, for the cruel, heartless, idiotic men who live there,* Cassandra added to herself.

"Really? Well, I am certain that you are happy to be back home in a civilized country again, my dear. Do enjoy yourself," Lady Debenham said before turning to greet her next guests.

Cassandra allowed herself to be led through to the other side of the ballroom, where Aunt Bradmore found some empty chairs.

It amazed Cassandra how familiar all of this was. Aside from the lack of flowers and the fewer number of officers, everything at this ball looked identical to the balls in Calcutta. She marveled once more at how hard the Englishwomen in Calcutta had worked to maintain everything the same as it was in England.

It was only the smell of those wonderful Indian flowers that was lacking. She twitched her nose as she passed by a particularly heady fragrance emanating from a lady dressed all in gold.

It was such a shame that English flowers did not smell as strong as those grown in India. This ballroom could certainly do with some.

Cassandra could not stop herself from looking around for a familiar dark head.

She shook her head. She was being ridiculous. Julian wasn't here. He was thousands of miles away in Calcutta.

An ache clutched at her heart. The ache was duller now, so much duller.

Throughout her first two weeks on the ship, the pain had kept her in her bed. But then, slowly, over time, she had been able to get up, to deal with the heartbreak from Julian's deception. It had begun to lessen on the ship, but still it was not entirely gone.

Cassandra wondered if it would ever completely go away.

But today she was beginning a different campaign—

one that would make up for all the heartache and melancholy that she had experienced over the last year.

She was here to attract attention—and not just anybody's attention. Like most of the other young, unmarried girls here, she wanted to attract the attention of the most handsome, eligible, and powerful gentlemen.

Only, she didn't want to marry them.

She wanted to use them.

She unfurled her fan and waved it vigorously in front of her face. Just look, she thought, at all of these men smiling and laughing with the young ladies here. How many hearts were going to be toyed with tonight? How many girls would fall in love, only to have that tender emotion hang unrequited, or worse, for their hearts to be cruelly broken as hers had been?

"Psst! Cassandra!" Olivia leaned across her mother, pulling Cassandra away from her unpleasant thoughts. "Remember to be languid, relaxed." Olivia gave Cassandra's fan a meaningful look.

Right. Olivia had schooled Cassandra on looking at ease earlier that week. Since she was determined to become an incomparable, she had to not only look the part—thus their many expeditions to the modiste's—she had to act the part.

Cassandra immediately schooled her face into one of impassivity and boredom and began to wave her fan lazily back and forth in front of her.

Dear Olivia was so much better at giving instructions than at carrying them out herself, Cassandra noticed, sliding her eyes over to look at her friend.

Olivia was sitting at the edge of her chair, looking around the room eagerly. Cassandra smiled, breaking her mask of languidness—Olivia looked rather like a bird of prey scouting out its next meal. Her thin, hawk-like face was intent and her eyes darted around here and there.

However, Olivia's advice did seem to work, for very soon a gentleman sauntered up to them and bowed to Lady Bradmore.

"Dear Lady Bradmore, you *must* introduce me to this beautiful young lady," the tall, thin gentleman said, taking Cassandra's hand.

Cassandra had to resist the urge to snatch her hand back. After all, wasn't this was what she wanted, male attention?

Her heart began to beat faster. How many hearts had this horrid creature broken?

Cassandra forced a small smile on to her lips. It was a very practiced smile, but she hoped it would be good enough to fool the gentleman who was now looking at her with such warm interest.

"But of course, your grace. Cassandra, this is the Duke of Hawksmore. Your grace, my niece, Miss Cassandra Renwick," Aunt Bradmore said, as the duke bowed and kissed Cassandra's hand. "And, of course, you remember my daughter, Olivia?"

The duke hardly took his eyes from Cassandra as he acknowledged Olivia. Cassandra, on her part, did her best to remain poised, keeping her precise smile on her face and trying not to appear either too excited to meet a duke nor too languid lest he think less of her.

A duke? This was perfect! He must be quite a catch!

"It is a striking gown you are wearing, Miss Renwick. Dare I assume that you have recently come from India?"

Cassandra had almost forgotten that she was wearing one of her new dresses. She had had a few new gowns made from the saris she had brought back from Calcutta.

She had designed the dress herself, to look almost as if she were wearing a sari, complete with the part that went over the shoulder and hung down her back. She was very pleased with the way it had turned out. It was certainly the most elegant dress she had ever owned, and it had gotten quite a few looks already this evening.

"It would be the most obvious assumption, your grace, and of course, a correct one. My parents are in Calcutta, where my father is working with the Governor-General."

"In that case, we should count ourselves very lucky to have you here in London."

"Thank you, sir." She tried to look demure, lowering her eyes.

The opening strains of the cotillion were played by the orchestra and guests began to crowd the floor for the dance.

"Miss Renwick, would you honor me with a dance?" The duke held out his arm, which, after permission was given by Lady Bradmore, Cassandra took with a quick backward glance of triumph to Olivia.

From that moment on, Cassandra was barely given an opportunity to rest. So many gentlemen, only some of whom she had met during her first, very brief, season the previous June, requested introductions—and all of them requested a dance.

She worked very hard to remain as amusing and alluring as she could, while still appearing to be the sweet, innocent girl that she was. She truly was, she thought, cut out for the stage.

No one was surprised by the number of bouquets of flowers that covered every possible space in the drawing room the following day.

The only thing that marred Cassandra's joy in her social success was that Lord Felbridge wasn't there to see it. After making her the laughingstock of society and breaking her heart, it would have been perfect if he could see just how popular she was now.

"Cassandra, how can you even think of Lord Felbridge at a time like this? You have become an incomparable overnight!"

"But that is the whole point, Olivia. I wanted the social success only so that I could show him just what he lost," Cassandra said, plucking at a soft pink rose.

"That is why you wanted to become a success? For revenge?" Olivia asked. Her eyes revealed her surprise.

Cassandra supposed that Olivia had thought that she wanted to attract gentlemen so that she could marry one. But then Olivia did not know all that Cassandra had been through. She was going to learn.

"Yes!" Cassandra said, whirling around toward Olivia. "Revenge!"

She began to move around the room, plucking petals from flowers here and there. "I want revenge. I want Lord Felbridge to kick himself for passing me up. To drown himself in brandy because he caused me to leave London, instead of marrying me on the spot. I want him to rue the day he ever toyed with Cassandra Renwick!" She snapped off the head of an expensive tulip.

Olivia was speechless.

"That is a very dangerous game to play, my dear," Lady Bradmore said, coming into the room.

Looking about at the petals strewn everywhere and at the decapitated tulip in Cassandra's hand, she said, "You must be very careful when trying to bring down an esteemed member of the *ton* like Lord Felbridge. He is a well-respected man and you, despite your success last night, are still new to society and in a very tenuous situation."

Aunt Bradmore plucked a red rose petal from the arm of the sofa she had sat down on and fingered its softness, releasing its gentle fragrance into the air.

"Your dowry makes you eligible to make your bow to the *beau monde*, Cassandra," she said. "And your father's position in the East India Company is excellent. But you are still the daughter of a baronet. I am sorry, my dear, but you would do better to play it safe. Enjoy your popularity and use it to find a good husband, but I would not push it further than that."

Cassandra tossed the tulip on to the table in front of her. "You may be right, Aunt, but I am afraid I cannot follow your advice. I am going to continue with my campaign and we will see what comes of it."

"Very well, Cassandra. But remember, it is your neck."

15

Green. Everywhere Julian looked there was green, from the rolling hillsides he passed along the road from Portsmouth to London, to the trees that lined the road and that were even abundant in the city itself. Julian was enthralled with the lush green beauty that was England.

What he couldn't figure out was how all this greenery survived the cool, damp weather. He was very happy that he had brought his overcoat with him. He had assumed he would need it on the ship, but never had he thought that he would need it during the day at the height of summer in England. But without it, he was much too cold.

He was equally dismayed by the fact that everything was much more expensive than he had anticipated. As he contemplated the very few coins left in his purse after paying for the post-chaise to carry him to London, he realized that his first stop had best be to the solicitors who were handling his father's estate.

Through most of the swaying carriage ride, his mind had been full of images of Cassandra and how surprised she would be to see him here.

Without a doubt, she would be thrilled to see him. He could clearly imagine her shock and how she would throw her arms around his neck, exclaiming at how he had followed her to England.

Surely, knowing of his deep love for her, she would immediately forgive him for initially having had baser intentions.

However, the closer they got to London, other worries began seep into his happy thoughts. What sort of reception would he be likely to receive from others who did not know him? It was certain that he would be treated with respect now that he was an earl. Wealth and title were all that mattered in society.

A small niggling doubt tickled the back of his mind, but his natural confidence easily squashed it. He would command the respect that he knew he deserved—just so long as he did not make any major social slips along the way.

He awoke from his reverie to find the carriage stopping before an unassuming building housing the firm of Strump, Strump, and Whitiker. Not wanting to take any chances on being denied his inheritance, Julian had brought with him as many pieces of identification as he could find. He now carefully carried the precious, battered tin box into the building.

Four men were sitting at a row of tall desks, copying out documents in the small room. Each one stopped what they were doing to stare at him.

It was the way he looked, of course, he thought to himself. Upon landing, he had realized at once that his clothing, which had even been a little out of fashion in Calcutta, was even more sadly out of style here.

He squared his shoulders, however, and approached the clerk closest to the door. "I am here to see Mr. Josiah Strump."

The man, who was nearly as young as Julian himself, looked down his nose and sneered, "Do you 'ave an appointment?"

"No, but you may tell him that the Earl of Huntley is here to see him," he loftily informed the impertinent man.

The man sniggered as he climbed off his stool and said, "I'll tell 'im."

Julian nodded, gave the other clerks his haughtiest stare and then sat down in the chair provided for clients.

Twenty minutes later Julian was still waiting and beginning to lose patience.

He stood up and approached the clerk once more. "Did you inform Mr. Strump that I was here and waiting for him?"

"Yes, I did. 'E'll see you when 'e's ready."

"That is unacceptable. He will see me now!" Julian strode past the clerk's desk with the intention of going straight into the office into which he had seen the clerk disappear earlier.

The man, however, cut him off. "I'll tell 'im you're still waiting', Mr. er . . . m'lord." With a shake of his head, he knocked gently at the door and went in, closing it behind him.

Julian went back to his chair and waited, tapping his foot.

Another ten minutes passed before an elderly man with bushy gray eyebrows finally emerged from the office. He came up to Julian and peered at him over his spectacles. "Lord Huntley?"

Julian stood. "Yes."

The man held out a gnarled hand and said, "Josiah Strump."

Julian shook his hand and then followed him back to his office.

Mr. Strump politely, if rather coldly, indicated that Julian should sit in the chair across from his large desk. He then sat down himself and stared at Julian.

"I am here about my father's inheritance. I was sorry to have missed the man you sent to Calcutta, but he did not stay very long—less than a day," Julian explained hesitantly, wondering why the man did nothing.

Mr. Strump cleared his throat. "Er, yes, yes. Well, he had other business to attend to. Other people to see in the country, you know." He mumbled something to himself that sounded like "Quite amazing."

He then seemed to recall himself to the matter at hand and unerringly pulled out a sheaf of papers from a huge and seemingly haphazard stack on one corner of the desk. Thumbing through the sheaf, he found one paper in particular and, with a wheezy sigh of satisfaction, sat back and got directly to business.

"I presume you have brought sufficient proof that you are who you say you are. Could I have a look at your papers?"

Julian unlocked his box and then handed it over.

"Er, thank you," the solicitor said, beginning to shuffle through the contents. "Although I am sure that no one could possibly mistake you, could they now, heh?" As he perused the papers, he chuckled to himself at his own joke.

Julian watched anxiously as the solicitor pored over the many letters he had brought with him. The longer the solicitor took, the more he worried he became that he had not brought enough, or possibly not the correct ones.

Mr. Strump, seeing his expression, mistook his concerns. "Surely you have seen a likeness of your father and noted your resemblance?"

Julian looked up from the box and into the old man's keen eyes. "No, as a matter of fact, I have never seen a likeness of my father. I believe my mother has one, but she never shared it with me. And I was too young when he left to remember what he looked like."

Julian wondered what this had to do with his papers, but supposed that the man was just trying to be friendly, especially after his cold reception.

"Oh! Well, I can assure you, if it were not for your, ah, coloring, you would be his spitting image," Mr. Strump explained, flushing an unbecoming deep red. His hands shook slightly as he shuffled the papers again and cleared his throat.

"Are the papers in order?" Julian asked, trying to remind the solicitor of his purpose for being there.

The solicitor looked at Julian, surprised. "Oh, of

course, my lord. Yes, yes, these should be sufficient to prove things beyond a doubt." The man put all the papers back into the box and leaned back in his chair once again. "That is not to say that you will not encounter any difficulties."

"What sort of difficulties?"

"Ah, well, you see, er . . ." Mr. Strump cleared his throat and looked back at the box on his desk.

"Well, of course, the problem is that no one really knows about you," Mr. Strump began hesitantly. "Your father never . . ."

"He never told anyone about his marriage to an Indian woman and that he had had a son by her," Julian said quietly, looking down at his hands.

He had expected this. This was why he had never been allowed to come to England. His father had probably been too embarrassed to admit to his marriage.

Well, it was just something that he was going to have to deal with. It was going to be awkward, but so had most of his life been awkward. It was nothing new, nothing he wasn't already used to dealing with. At least now he had a title and wealth, so it shouldn't be too difficult.

He looked up, forcing a smile onto his face. "Well, I suppose in that case it is a good thing that I look like my father. And certainly, once people know who I am, there should be no difficulties."

"Er, ah, yes," the solicitor said uncertainly.

"Very good. Then there is only one other thing," Julian said uncertainly.

Mr. Strump gave him a wary look.

"I, ah, was not able to bring a great deal of money with me on the journey. I needed, of course, to leave my mother most of what I had on hand so that she could continue to live comfortably until I am able to send her more."

Mr. Strump looked very relieved and even managed a small smile. "My lord, you should have no concerns about money. You are now quite a wealthy man. I can advance you all that you may need for the moment and give you the name and direction of your father's banker."

"Thank you." He hadn't thought it would be a problem, but he had not been entirely sure how the issue would be received. It was a great relief that it was so easily taken care of.

Mr. Strump jotted down a name and address on a piece of paper, then reached into the drawer directly in front of him and pulled out a small leather bag. He handed it to Julian along with the piece of paper. "I hope that this should suffice for the time being."

Julian felt the heavy weight of the bag in his hand. He was certain he would not need nearly so much money in the immediate future. However, he pocketed the bag and stood up to leave.

"Thank you," he said again.

"Of course, and if you need anything else, do not hesitate to ask. Your father was one of my oldest clients. I am sorry for your loss."

Cassandra convinced Lord Hawksmore to sit out his promised dance with her that evening. As much as she loved to dance, she still needed some time to rest. She knew that the duke would be happy to comply, as he was with everything she asked of him.

The past week had been thrilling for Cassandra. So far, her plan to become the toast of society was working like a charm. She had a string of beaus surrounding her at every party, and the duke was always sure to be one of them. Now all she needed was for Lord Felbridge to turn up, so that she could lure him to her side as well and then exact her revenge on him.

Lord Hawksmore and she had not been speaking for more than five minutes when a buzz spread through the ballroom. The duke stopped in mid-sentence and they both looked up.

Everyone was bowing low to welcome the Prince

Regent. Prinny graciously stopped to speak with his host and hostess, standing not too far from Cassandra. From what she could see, he was all that she had heard and more.

He had such character! He spoke loudly so that everyone could hear and was clothed spectacularly in a black coat with silver embroidery all over it, and matching breeches.

Cassandra was, as everyone else, completely speechless in his magnificent presence. She was also very happy that she had elected to wear her own best sari-dress, the one made from the turquoise sari which she had bought because it was the same color as Julian's eyes.

How she had wished Julian could have seen her in all her glory! His expressive eyes, which had been so filled with love for her, shimmered in front of her mind's eye. There was not a day that went by that she did not think of him, and the dull ache in her heart was a constant reminder of his betrayal.

And it constantly renewed her determination to play her game of revenge.

"One must be introduced to the most beautiful young ladies present, my lord," Prinny was saying to Lord Roseberry, their host that evening.

There was a titter among the young ladies and their mamas, wondering who among them Lord Roseberry would introduce to the prince. Everyone wanted to be introduced, and more than one lady with a daughter in tow attempted to get Lord Roseberry's attention by fluttering her fan, waving her fan, opening and closing her fan—any stratagem at all to catch his eye.

Cassandra could not help but giggle.

Lord Hawksmore leaned toward her. "Miss Renwick, I cannot imagine what you find so amusing! Please do enlighten me," he said, smiling at her, eager to share the joke.

"It is just the fluttering of fans, your grace. The room

has cooled down so very quickly that I am sorry I do not have my wrap with me."

Lord Hawksmore's bark of laughter caught the prince's attention as he was about to be introduced to Miss Georgina Scott, the reigning incomparable of the season.

Immediately, and without a backward glance, he abandoned poor Miss Scott, her hand still held out for the royal touch.

"Hawksmore," the prince said, coming over to them. "You must share the joke. But first introduce us to this lovely Indian princess you have with you."

Lord Hawksmore bowed low to Prinny, and then introduced him to Cassandra, who was suddenly having the most difficult time breathing.

"From whence in India did you come, Miss Renwick?" His Royal Highness asked.

"From Calcutta, sir, where my father is working with Lord Minto."

"Ah, Minto. Yes, yes, how is the old boy? Things going well over there?"

"Very well, sir, and Lord Minto is doing wonderful things, from what I understand. I had the pleasure of meeting him on quite a few occasions."

"Good, good. We applaud your style, Miss Renwick, and your beauty. Will you dance?"

"Th-thank you, sir, I would be honored."

With a nod from the prince, the orchestra struck up a country dance, and His Royal Highness led Cassandra out on to the floor.

Cassandra was certain she was going faint. Not only was she having trouble breathing, but now everything seemed to have become fuzzy around the edges. Still, she kept a smile on her face and followed Prinny in the steps of the dance.

If there was any question at all about her social position up until now, it was most assuredly put to rest. If only Lord Felbridge could see her now!

She looked around the room, but he was still nowhere

to be seen. She would have to ask around to find out if he was even in town.

She nearly laughed. Lord Felbridge had said she wasn't good enough for him. And here she was, dancing with the prince. If this didn't prove how frivolous society was, nothing did.

Cassandra held her head up high and sought to entertain the prince as best she could. But she was surprised when he turned the tables and began to entertain her.

She laughed as he recalled for her the most recent witticisms of his good friend Beau Brummell. In fact, she was laughing so hard that by the end of the dance she nearly missed her cue to curtsey.

"Thank you, Your Royal Highness, for a dance I shall remember my whole life. You are exceedingly gracious," Cassandra said, as she sank into her curtsey.

The prince looked especially pleased with this and gave her a slight nod of his head before going off to seek other amusements.

Lady Bradmore and Olivia were by her side within a blink of her eye.

"My dear, your reputation is made! You will be the talk of the *ton* for at least the next two weeks, if not longer!" Aunt Bradmore gushed.

"Oh Cassandra, how lucky you are!" cooed Olivia.

But all Cassandra could do was smile.

16

Cassandra tried to peer over the head of the gentleman sitting next to her on the soft blanketed grass. Over the past week, she had been to more soirees, breakfasts and musicales than she could ever remember attending. Lady Bradmore had suddenly been swamped with invitations.

But there was still no sign of Lord Felbridge.

> *"Your eyes, like limpid pools of blue*
> *Lure my confession I love you . . ."*

Mr. Cawfield declaimed, reciting his latest poem, cleverly entitled "Cassandra of my Heart."

Was Lord Felbridge somehow aware of what she was doing and deliberately avoiding her?

> *"Our two sweet souls should never part*
> *Dearest Cassandra of my heart."*

He finished in a grand and deliberate manner, ending with a flourish, with his hand coming to rest against his bulging stomach.

Cassandra looked at his hand and raised her own to her lips to swallow back her laughter.

"Er . . ." Mr. Cawfield quickly moved his hand up to his chest and flushed.

"That was lovely, truly it was. I am quite touched."

The man stammered and turned an even deeper shade of pink. But before he could say anything Cassandra said, "It is so wonderful to see so many people here today. Mrs. Price-Liste must be thrilled at the number of people in attendance. For a Venetian breakfast it is rather unusual, is it not?"

Mr. Cawfield looked around at the crowded garden in a rather crestfallen way. "Yes, quite."

"You haven't seen Lord Felbridge recently, have you?" Cassandra asked, as innocuously as she could.

"Er, no. Bit out of my league," Mr. Cawfield said, ducking his head.

"Oh, yes, I understand," Cassandra reached out and touched his arm. "I truly liked the poem, though."

The gentleman immediately colored again. "Th . . . thank you, Miss Renwick."

"Cousin, my mother has requested that you join her," Charles, Lord Bradmore, interrupted, looking pointedly at her hand resting on Mr. Cawfield's arm.

She stood up immediately and Mr. Cawfield somehow ended up in a coughing fit. "You will excuse me, Mr. Cawfield?"

He nodded, unable to speak for the moment.

She followed her cousin toward Lady Bradmore.

"I do hope that you aren't deliberately encouraging that scrounger?" her cousin asked with an exaggerated shudder.

"Oh no. But he is so earnest in his adulation, I could not turn him away. And besides, he had written a poem for me."

She received a sidelong glance of disbelief from her cousin. Cassandra giggled. "It was very thoughtful of him. Not a very good poem, but very thoughtful nonetheless."

"There you are, Cassandra. I did not know where you had disappeared to," Aunt Bradmore said, even though she did not look overly concerned. Olivia was seated next to her on the pretty wrought-iron bench.

"Mr. Cawfield was reciting a poem he had written for me."

"Cawfield wrote a poem, did you say?" They were joined by Charles's friend, Mr. St. John Fotheringay-Phipps. Known to all simply as Fungy, he was the best-dressed gentleman of the *ton*—aside from Beau Brummell, of course. Today he was resplendent in a dark green coat and fawn pantaloons, with a neckcloth that must have taken hours to tie, so complicated was the knot.

"He was certainly making some grand gestures when I came over," Charles said, quirking up one side of his mouth.

Cassandra laughed. "Oh yes, he was very grand with his gestures. The poem itself was . . . tolerable."

"Bad as that, eh?" Fungy said. "Must say, I never heard that Cawfield was a poet. You, Merry?" Mr. Fotheringay-Phipps turned to his ever-present cousin, Lord Merrick. The two were rarely ever seen apart, although Cassandra supposed it did happen on occasion.

"No. Doesn't surprise me, though. I believe Miss Renwick has turned a number of erstwhile gentlemen into poets recently. One of the hazards of being an incomparable, Miss Renwick," Lord Merrick said, giving her a broad smile and a small bow.

Cassandra shrugged her shoulders. "It will be difficult to live with, but I shall suffer through somehow," she teased.

"Suffer is bang on the mark, Miss Renwick, with Cawfield spouting poetry at you," Fungy said.

"I heard you were asking after Lord Felbridge, Miss Renwick," Lord Merrick said.

Charles looked at Cassandra quizzically. She had heard from Olivia that he had been very surprised by his friend's treatment of her last summer and had even gone so far as to avoid Lord Felbridge because of it.

"Yes," Cassandra said, avoiding Charles's eye. "I was

just wondering where he was, since I haven't seen him since I've returned."

"Why would you be interested, Cousin?" Charles asked pointedly.

"Oh, I, er, I was just curious is all." Cassandra shrugged as if it was of no importance.

"Heard he was in the country. Isn't that what Elsworth said?" Fungy asked Lord Merrick.

"Yes, but I believe he'll be returning to London soon. If I see him, shall I mention that you were looking for him, Miss Renwick?"

"Oh no!" She quickly moderated her voice. "No, thank you so much, my lord. There is no need to do that. I am certain I shall run into him sometime." No need to push things, she thought to herself.

Julian was thrilled to be in London. He couldn't have been in a better position—he was wealthy, titled, young and, if he did say so himself, rather handsome. He would have to beat the ladies off with a stick, he thought, laughing to himself.

His days of hanging on the edges of society were gone. They were done. He was now going to be welcomed wherever he went, invited to every party, and should have no problems getting young ladies to dance with him.

One young lady figured in his mind the most.

Cassandra.

The only possible problem he would have with her was if she was still angry with him for playing that game with her. But she would be so happy to see him, he was certain she would forgive him right away.

But first, he would enter society, make his name known and take his seat in Parliament. Julian had to suppress a smile at this thought—who would ever have thought that a Eurasian would sit in Parliament! Well, for that matter, whoever had thought there would be one in the *beau monde?*

And yet here he was, ready to begin his life as a peer of the realm.

He had learned that the fashionable hour to be out and about was at four. So soon after that hour he ventured out for a stroll among the *beau monde*. It was only then that he realized that perhaps things would not be quite as easy as he had thought.

The number of people crowding the pathways through the park astounded Julian. It seemed as if the whole population of London were out walking, riding horses or driving in carriages. They greeted each other, calling or waving, stopping their carriages for a quick chat and holding up the whole line behind them.

Everyone knew everyone else, but there was not one person known to Julian, and he felt it.

This was almost worse than being in Calcutta. At least there he knew the people who were cutting him. Here, he was cut left and right by people he had never seen before.

It wasn't even so much that they cut him. It was more that they did not actually see him.

No one met his eye.

He tried doffing his hat to a couple of ladies who walked past him, but they ignored him. He bowed to a very grand looking lady and gentleman in a barouche passing by, but they did not even look his way.

Even when he stopped in the middle of the path, blocking the way for the people behind him, they just walked around him as if he wasn't there.

Julian was at a standstill. Literally and figuratively. He just did not know what to do. How did one meet people? He was sure that if he just met someone, anyone, then he could meet others and then everything would be all right. But how did one begin?

"Pardon me?"

Julian turned around, startled that someone was actually speaking to him. But then he realized that the gentleman must just want to get by him on the path.

Julian gave the man a small bow. "I am terribly sorry,"

he said, and then stepped onto the grass so that the man could pass.

But the man, who was clearly dressed in the height of fashion, did not pass him. Instead he looked at him, no, he stared at him through a quizzing glass that he wore around his neck on a bright red ribbon.

Julian could not help but stare back. He looked exactly like a fashion plate from a magazine—handsome, with a well sculpted face, carefully tousled brownish-blond hair and a neckcloth tied in a style that Julian could never dream of achieving.

"You look very familiar. Have we met?" the gentleman asked slowly.

"I do not believe so, sir. I have recently come from India." Julian held out his hand. "Julian Ritchie, er, Earl of Huntley," he added awkwardly.

"St. John Fotheringay-Phipps, at your service." The exquisite bowed after shaking Julian's hand. "Believe I knew your father."

"Really?"

"Looked exactly like you, only older and, er, fairer."

Julian laughed. "Yes, naturally."

Mr. Fotheringay-Phipps looked him over again with his spectacle. "How recent is recently?" he asked obscurely.

"What? Oh, just arrived in London yesterday, in Portsmouth a little over a week ago," Julian answered, beginning to feel like he was under some sort of microscope.

"Met your aunt and Bradmore yet?" Mr. Fotheringay-Phipps asked, dropping his quizzing glass.

Julian was confused. "My aunt? I was not aware . . . oh wait, yes, of course! My father mentioned that he had a sister who was rather high in the instep."

Mr. Fotheringay-Phipps laughed. "Yes, that would be Lady Bradmore. Exceedingly conscious of her social position, as well as everyone else's. But really, very kind lady, y'know."

"Oh, I am terribly sorry, I didn't mean . . ."

"No, that is quite all right. Can say anything you want about her. Not my aunt."

Julian smiled. "Yes. You wouldn't happen to know her direction, would you?"

"Number 30, St. James Square. Believe she'll be 'at home' tomorrow."

Julian nodded, committing the address to memory. "I am sorry to trouble you, but perhaps you could tell me an appropriate time to call. I am just coming to realize that we keep very different hours in Calcutta."

"Of course, not at all. Two in the afternoon would be about right." Mr. Fotheringay-Phipps paused. "Haven't met your cousin, then?" he asked.

"My cousin? I didn't know I had one," Julian said, growing more and more pleased as he learned more about his family.

"Charles Bradmore," Mr. Fotheringay-Phipps said shortly. "Has a sister as well," he continued, "Miss Olivia Bradmore, lovely girl. Very soft-hearted and gentle."

"I look forward to meeting them." Julian held out his hand once more to the gentleman. "Thank you so much for the information. I do hope we have the opportunity to meet again."

Mr. Fotheringay-Phipps grasped his fingers gently. "Pleasure," he said and then lounged off, walking with the most bored air Julian could possibly imagine. Julian had a hard time not laughing, but he did not think that would be polite.

He then noticed that other people had begun to look at him. All of a sudden he existed to them. He wondered what had changed.

He lifted his hat to a woman who stared at him through her quizzing-glass. Passing by in a black barouche, she and her companion immediately put their heads together and began talking excitedly to each other.

Julian just smiled. Well, he supposed it was better to be noticed and gossiped about than not to be noticed at all.

* * *

Cassandra was in the position she had always dreamed of—admittedly, it was not one she had ever thought would actually happen. Her cousin's drawing room held a good number of gentlemen, many of whom were surrounding her, trying to outwit each other while hanging on her every word.

It was incredible what a little attention from the right people could do for one's social position.

"Miss Renwick, you must be so happy to be home again after the horrors of Calcutta," Crusty Corstairs said, voicing the sentiment which had been repeated too many times already.

Cassandra sighed. "There was no horror there, Mr. Corstairs. The English there live exactly the same way as we do here, which I must say, I found a little ridiculous."

"But the natives and the diseases, Miss Renwick. I have heard terrible stories," Lord Bertram said from her other side.

"There are diseases, horrible diseases, my lord. And there are natives, of course, but you should not equate one with the other." Cassandra really did not like getting into political discussions with these gentlemen. They knew so little about which they spoke, and yet could lecture for hours.

"Tell me, Lord Merrick, how are the plans for your mother's archery party coming along?" Cassandra asked the very tall and incredibly handsome marquis, who was always seen with the most fashionable young ladies and yet had never gotten trapped by one, and who, for once, was without his cousin, Mr. Fotheringay-Phipps.

"Very well, Miss Renwick. I know you are going to thoroughly enjoy yourself there. You are planning on attending, are you not?"

"Most definitely, my lord, only . . ."

"Only? Miss Renwick, is there something in particular you would like at the party? If it is within my power, you know that I shall attain it for you," he said, leaning forward toward her.

Cassandra giggled. "Oh no, sir, it is only that I never learned archery." She looked up at him from under her eyelashes and batted them innocently.

He smiled. "I will be more than honored if you would allow me to teach you."

"You are too kind, my lord," Cassandra said, holding back more giggles. "Now this is a much more pleasant conversation, gentlemen. Or is it a flirtation?" she asked, looking around at the other men standing by her.

Lord Merrick laughed, although some of the other gentlemen did not. They only managed to look daggers at Merrick, who had succeeded in amusing Cassandra when they had not.

"It is most definitely a flirtation, Miss Renwick, and a very enjoyable one as well, despite the crowd," his lordship said, taking her hand and placing a light kiss on the back of it.

"I say! Merrick, you are not the only man speaking with Miss Renwick, and you'd be good to remember that," Mr. Corstairs objected.

"Mr. Corstairs, it is perfectly all right. I beg you please, do not get put out by Lord Merrick's gallantry. Perhaps after his lordship shows me the basics of archery, you could give me some pointers? I am certain you are an excellent shot," Cassandra said, tilting her head to one side hopefully.

Mr. Corstairs ran his hand through his bright red hair. "Yes, as a matter of fact, I am."

It was at that moment that she felt as if someone had just stuck a knife between her ribs and straight into her heart.

17

Between Lord Merrick and Mr. Corstairs, Cassandra could see Julian standing just inside the door. He was staring at her with a confused expression on his face. He clenched his strong jaw and his hands rolled themselves up into fists.

Cassandra blinked and shook her head. She had to be imagining this. Julian wasn't here in London. He was in Calcutta. She looked at Lord Merrick, who suddenly was looking very concerned.

"Miss Renwick, are you all right?" He took hold of her elbow in case she should swoon. It was a good thing he did, because she was feeling remarkably lightheaded all of a sudden.

"I . . ." she looked to him for support and a strong dose of reality. "Yes, I am fine. I am terribly sorry, Mr. Corstairs, did you say something?"

"Who *is* that?" Lord Bertram asked, also staring at Julian.

"Do you know that gentleman, Miss Renwick?" Lord Merrick asked.

Cassandra looked back at Julian, who had now turned his attention to Aunt Bradmore. Her aunt looked a little discomfited, but was speaking with Julian in a gracious way. She led him further into the room and toward her son.

"Miss Renwick?"

She turned back to Lord Merrick. "I am sorry, my lord, do I know him? Ah, yes, as a matter of fact, I do. He is someone I knew in Calcutta, which is why I am so surprised to see him here."

She turned to look at the other gentlemen around her, none of whom looked very happy with her reaction to Julian's arrival. "I am terribly sorry, gentlemen, what were we talking about?"

The men resumed their conversation about archery, but Cassandra could not stay focused on what they were saying. Her eyes kept straying back to Julian.

What was he doing here? How did he get here? He could not, would not have followed her, would he? Surely he had achieved his goal of thoroughly humiliating her, of proving he could make an English woman fall in love with a Eurasian? Why would he come to England after that?

Had he followed her?

So many questions ran through her mind. So much pain welled up in her heart and began to churn up into her throat. There was a bitter taste in her mouth as she watched Julian talking first with Charles and then with Olivia.

And yet, seeing him was like a balm to her agitated emotions. Had she somehow forgotten how handsome he was, or was it just that she had not seen him for so long? He was smiling encouragingly at Olivia as she spoke to him.

And there was something else that was different about him. He had vitality. Among so many gentlemen who worked hard at presenting an air of boredom, Julian was wonderfully, brightly alive and quick. He spoke quickly, and he looked alert and interested in everything that was going on around him.

How she loved him!

No! Where had that thought come from?

Yes, he was handsome, he had always been so. But watching him, smiling and chatting amiably with her cousin and best friend, she felt the same heat and shortness of breath as she had after he had last kissed her by the shore of the Hooghly River in Calcutta.

How could that be? How could she still feel that way? He had betrayed her, he had toyed with her and used her. She hated him!

And he was coming over to her!

"Cassandra, Lord Huntley says that he is a friend of yours from Calcutta," Lady Bradmore said, smiling graciously from Cassandra to Julian. Olivia stood next to her mother, looking very expectant, like a dog being offered a bone.

Cassandra blinked. "Lord Huntley?"

"Well, in Calcutta, Miss Renwick knew me as Mr. Ritchie," Julian said, looking at her as if he were trying to read her mind.

"Oh yes, of course!" Lady Bradmore said, "But now you are the Earl of Huntley, naturally."

"An earl? I'm sorry, I didn't know," Cassandra heard herself saying.

"Yes, my father died a short time ago. I received word of it the very same day you left Calcutta," he said gently in a voice tinged with pain.

This caught Cassandra by surprise. Was he hurt when she had left? If so, then he deserved it for breaking her heart. Or was the sorrow she had heard in his voice at the loss of his father?

Cassandra desperately wished she could know what he was thinking.

"I am sorry to hear about your father. Although it is wonderful that you are here now, and an earl, my goodness! My mother must have been quite shocked to hear of this."

Julian laughed, and a true smile brightened his turquoise eyes. "Unfortunately, I did not take the time to inform her myself, although, as you can imagine, I would have loved to have seen her reaction."

Cassandra shared a secret smile with him, both of them knowing exactly what her mother's reaction would have been. Cassandra could just imagine the growls of denial that would have come from her.

Olivia's large curious eyes caught Cassandra's for a moment. As usual, nothing got past her friend's notice. Olivia may have generally been a quiet person, but she noticed everything. There would be explanations to make later, Cassandra was certain.

"Ah, Huntley, made it, did you?" Fungy said, coming up to them.

Julian turned around and held out his hand to him. "Yes, thank you so much. I am glad to meet you again." He turned to Lady Bradmore. "It was Mr. Fotheringay-Phipps who gave me your direction, Aunt Bradmore."

"No problem, no problem at all," Fungy drawled languidly.

Julian's lips twitched as he experienced the full glory that was Fungy.

Looking at Fungy standing next to Julian truly made it more than obvious to Cassandra just how out of fashion Julian was, in both his clothes and demeanor. Fungy was, as ever, dressed to perfection, wearing a dark blue super fine coat over a most handsomely embroidered waistcoat, and his white topped Hessians were so shiny, Cassandra thought she could see her reflection in them.

Julian, however, was wearing clothes Cassandra remembered very well. His outmoded jacket, breeches and brilliantly colored waistcoat looked even more out of place here than they had in Calcutta, and his boots had clearly seen better days.

Could it be this which made her love him all the more?

Cassandra scolded herself. No, she did not love him—she could not, not after the way he had behaved.

But she did, still, admire him. She admired the way he

stuck to his principles, and the way he did not let society's dictates sway him.

She admired the fact that he dared society to accept him for who he is, not what he wore. How she wished that she did not have to play her games, and that she could be more like him.

Julian's eyes had been drawn to Cassandra the minute he had walked into his aunt's drawing room. He had to work hard not to pull her from the knot of men who surrounded her.

Cassandra, *his* Cassandra, was laughing and flirting with other men!

It took some effort, but he calmed himself.

He supposed he shouldn't be at all surprised that she was surrounded by gentlemen. She had been so in Calcutta as well. But, he supposed, he had been rather hoping that she had been pining for him as he had been for her.

But clearly she had not missed him at all.

A spark of hope burned in him for a moment. Perhaps she had, indeed, missed him. Perhaps this was just her way of dealing with her heartbreak.

But another look at the gentlemen surrounding her quickly disabused him of this thought. They were all smartly dressed and clearly very amusing, as they had her laughing and flirting.

He had never felt more like a country bumpkin, so out of place and out of style.

He had thought it would be so easy to find Cassandra and win her heart back.

What, then, was the way back into her heart? Looking at Fungy's resplendence, he suddenly knew.

He had to become a gentleman of fashion in order to win her attention. If he wanted to be favored in her company, then he had to become more like his peers of the *beau monde*—more like her new beaus.

Once he had her attention, then, hopefully, her love would come along.

* * *

Julian looked around the comfortable private sitting room where he was eating his dinner. He had waited patiently for the past two days for his cousin Bradmore to contact him as he had promised, but so far there was no word from him.

Julian shrugged. He should have gone with his first instinct, that Bradmore had just said he would help out to be polite. He obviously had no intention of actually helping Julian.

But there was no reason for Julian to just sit around and wait for help to come to him. No, if he truly wanted to win Cassandra back, then he had to go out and solicit the help and guidance he needed.

If Bradmore wasn't going to provide any help, he knew who would.

It was less than an hour later that Julian was knocking on Fungy's door. It was opened by a rather diminutive, but very serious looking man.

"Is Mr. Fotheringay-Phipps in?" Julian asked.

"And you are?" the man asked, looking down his nose at him, as much as that was possible when Julian stood nearly a foot taller than the officious looking butler.

"Lord Huntley," Julian said, with much more ease than he had just two days ago. He was definitely getting used to his new title.

The man bowed him into a small hallway and then walked a few steps to the drawing room, where he indicated Julian should wait.

Fungy's drawing room was very comfortable, although it could have used an airing out. It was a bit stuffy and smelled a little like a combination of tobacco and soot from the fire. But for a bachelor gentleman's quarters, Julian supposed it was understandable.

He sat down in an overstuffed chair and then laughed

as he noticed that the newspapers, which were strewn all over the small table next to him, were all opened to the pages devoted to gossip and society *on-dits*.

He had just started to read that day's paper when the butler returned and requested that Julian follow him to "the master's chamber." Julian was rather surprised at the intimacy of this, but did as he was requested.

Fungy was standing in his bedchamber in his shirt-sleeves and a pair of buff-colored pantaloons, contemplating an array of waistcoats and coats which were laid out on his bed. He picked up a bright yellow waistcoat with blue flowers embroidered on it and put it next to a coat of pale yellow.

After contemplating that for a moment, he moved it next to a coat of deep green. Crossing his arms over his chest, he stood silently staring at the combination.

Suddenly he turned around, as if he had just remembered Julian's existence. "What do you think, old man, yellow or green? Yellow or green? Can't make up my mind."

Julian walked over, looked at the waistcoat, and said, "What about blue?"

Fungy looked horrified. "Can't do that! Wore that last week. No, it has to be either yellow or green."

"Oh, well, then, I'd say the green," Julian offered.

Fungy nodded sagely. "Yes, yellow it is."

Julian was confused for a moment, but then just laughed as Fungy put on the waistcoat and then went to contemplate the neckcloths his man was holding out for him to choose.

"Tricky business this, getting dressed," Fungy said seriously.

Julian began to laugh and then realized that his friend was not joking. He quickly turned his laugh into a cough. "Yes, I suppose so."

"Clearly, you are not so troubled by this as I am," Fungy said, critically eyeing Julian's clothes.

"Er, well, no. That is, actually, one thing I wished to speak to you about, if I may?" Julian started hesitantly.

A broad smile slowly spread across Fungy's face, and he paused as he was about to start the tricky business of tying his neckcloth. "Wondered when you'd come to me. Knew it would be sooner rather than later. Made an appointment for you with m'tailor for tomorrow at two."

"You did?" Julian was shocked. How had Fungy known that he would come to him for help about entering the world of fashion? And new clothes would certainly be the first step towards acceptance.

He was about to voice his question when Fungy's valet gave Julian a very stern look.

"Mr. Fotheringay-Phipps should *not* be disturbed or spoken to when he is tying," he whispered officiously.

Julian snapped his mouth closed and watched the complicated procedure silently. Twenty minutes and only five neckcloths later, the job was done to Fungy's satisfaction. Julian was impressed.

"What was the other thing you wished to see me about?" Fungy asked, allowing his valet to help him on with his coat.

Julian was caught off guard for a moment, but then remembered himself. "Well, I was just wondering how one got invited to society parties. How I could get to know people . . . you understand?

He paused awkwardly. "My cousin offered to take me about and introduce me, but so far has not called to follow through with his offer."

Fungy scowled. "Not surprised. Bradmore's a nice chap at times, but only when it is convenient for him." He then patted Julian on the back and led him back toward the drawing room.

"Not a problem. Be happy to introduce you. Got to have you rigged out first, though," he said, looking sadly once more at Julian's clothes.

A loud laugh greeted them as they entered the room. "You still going on about poor Huntley's clothes, Fungy?" Lord Merrick was sitting in one of the chairs with a drink in his hand, looking like he had been there a while.

"Well, Merry, you've got to admit . . ."

"Yes, they are sadly out of style. But honestly, Huntley, it is nothing that can't be easily fixed. Don't be put out by Fungy's nitpicking," Lord Merrick said.

Julian was taken aback by Lord Merrick's forthright speech as well as his ease of manner. They had very briefly met at Lady Bradmore's, and already he was speaking to him as if they were the best of friends. Julian gave him a hesitant smile.

"Going to put him up at White's. Second it?" Fungy asked Lord Merrick.

"Happy to!" he said, getting up and pouring a brandy from the decanter on a small side table.

Julian wondered if Lord Merrick always made himself so at home wherever he went. Fungy did not seem to have a problem with it. He was standing in front of the glass above the fireplace, looking questioningly at himself. He delicately ran his hand through the dark blond waves of his hair, carefully arranging it to his satisfaction.

"That is very good of you, my lord," Julian said, turning his attention back to Lord Merrick.

"No problem, and please, no 'my lords' here. I am Merry to my friends," he said, handing Julian the glass half filled with brandy.

Julian took a small sip, allowing the burning liquid to coat his tongue and the back of his throat.

"Only the best," Fungy said, watching him with a small smile playing on his lips.

Julian immediately was embarrassed at being caught savoring the brandy. "Oh, of course. It is just that we don't get much brandy in Calcutta. I believe I am developing quite a taste for it."

Fungy chuckled. "Excellent! Anything I can do to help you get acclimated."

Merry joined in his laughter, "Fungy, you are too good!"

"Yes, I am, aren't I?" Fungy replied, taking the compliment as his due. "And you don't know the half of it. Going to take him to my tailor tomorrow."

Merry raised his eyebrows. "You *are* good! I'll have you know, Huntley, that many a man would die to receive a word of fashion advice from Fungy."

"Really? Well, I readily believe that. Fungy is certainly the best-dressed gentleman I have seen so far. Er, no offense, my lord, er, Merry," Julian quickly remedied.

"No offense taken. It is perfectly true. We rather pride ourselves on Fungy's prowess in the dressing room!" Merry said and then burst out laughing again.

Julian could not hold back his own laughter at this, and even Fungy was amused, laughing with Merry and giving him a small bow in acceptance of his accolades.

Julian was amazed at the easy relationship between the men. They seemed to fit into each other's pocket without a thought or a hesitation.

Their easygoing manners and open offer of friendship was beyond what Julian could have possibly expected. He felt honored to have been taken up by them.

Merry gave Julian a rather embarrassed look. "You must excuse us, Huntley. We have a previously arranged dinner engagement."

"We'd ask you to join us, naturally—but not our party. You understand," Fungy finished for Merry.

"Oh, yes, that is not a problem. I did not mean to make you late," Julian said, putting down his glass.

"Not at all!" Fungy said, on his way out the door. He then turned back. "Pick you up a little before two tomorrow?"

"Yes, that would be wonderful," Julian said, truly looking forward to this special treat.

"Still at that hotel?"

"Gronow's, yes."

Fungy nodded with his eyebrows pulled down. "Must do something about that too."

And then he was out the door, with Merry following.

Within two weeks, Fungy had worked miracles.

To Julian's chagrin, he had five new waistcoats and five

more on order, three new coats and another four ordered, as well as breeches for evening wear, pantaloons for day wear, and neckcloths galore. He was awaiting his white-topped Hessians and his first pair of dancing slippers. Fungy had assured him he would need at least five pairs of these, as they wore out so quickly and, naturally, he would be dancing quite a bit once he had begun to receive invitations.

Oddly enough, all this reminded Julian of his youth in India. How hard he had tried to fit in with the English there! He had dressed in the height of Calcutta fashion, engaged in all the English sports, and done everything he could to be as English as anyone.

But it had not been worth the effort. There had been no discernable change in people's attitudes toward him, no matter what he wore or how he behaved.

But it absolutely had to work this time. At stake was not just respect from London society, but the heart of the woman he loved.

In addition to his new wardrobe, Julian now had rooms in the Albany, which he was assured was The Most Exclusive place for a bachelor to lodge. On Merry's advice, he had not requested that his father's town house be vacated by the current tenants, since only the stodgiest bachelors, or those out to catch a wife and set up their nurseries, lived in theirs.

Finally, his name had been put up for membership at two esteemed gentlemen's clubs, White's and Boodle's. He had joined Merry and Fungy for dinner at both of these clubs, so that the other gentlemen would have an opportunity to meet him. And he had an idea that both Fungy and Merry were waging an all-out campaign for ensuring his approval.

He, himself, was working toward the same end, and had hosted a number of gentlemen, including Fungy and Merry, for dinner at his hotel just before moving to his new rooms. It had been a late night, but a successful one.

Julian took the air each afternoon in Hyde Park and

managed to meet a number of ladies and gentlemen while walking or riding with Fungy or Merry, or, as was usually the case, both.

But so far, although he had been casually invited to a few dinner parties arranged at a club, no formal invitations had yet arrived for him. Neither Merry nor Fungy would comment on this when asked.

18

Cassandra aimed her arrow at the target at the other end of the field. Mr. Corstairs stood just behind her, steadying her arm with his hand.

He had just removed his hand when she heard someone call out behind her, "Felbridge! Finally back from rusticating, I see."

Her eyes hazed over with anger and she loosed the arrow.

"Well done, Miss Renwick! A bull's-eye. Amazing!" Mr. Corstairs took a step back and scratched his head.

"Very well done," Lord Merrick said. He stood just next to Mr. Corstairs, and had been giving Cassandra pointers as well.

Cassandra turned around to see Lord Felbridge looking with narrowed eyes at her arrow sitting dead center in the target.

"Well done, Miss Renwick. I didn't know you were an archer," he drawled as soon as he noticed that she was looking at him.

"Mr. Corstairs and Lord Merrick have been kind enough to teach me just today." She had to fight herself to keep from reaching for another arrow to put straight through his black heart.

Instead, if her plan was going to work, she had to force herself to be calm, even enticing.

Lord Felbridge nodded to Mr. Corstairs and Lord Merrick, who were both looking very pleased with their pupil.

She smiled warmly at Mr. Corstairs. "Shall I try again?"

"By all means, Miss Renwick. You seem to be taking to this very quickly."

"Yes, but I could not do it without your steadying hand, sir, if you don't mind," she said, flirting with him outrageously with her eyes. She then turned her back to him and let fly her arrow.

Lord Felbridge stayed to watch. When, once again, she hit the target straight in the center, he applauded with the other gentlemen.

Two other gentlemen joined them as she shot her third and fourth arrows. But after that she put down her bow. "I am sorry, gentlemen, I find I am in need of some refreshment. Archery can be a tiring sport."

Immediately, Mr. Corstairs and the Duke of Hawksmore stepped forward, declaring that they would be honored to obtain some lemonade for her.

"You are both too kind, but perhaps Lord Felbridge could do me the honor," she said, cocking her head at him and giving him her sweetest smile.

Lord Felbridge bowed and went off in search of her drink.

She suppressed her giggles at the thought that she now had Felbridge at her command.

Revenge could be so sweet.

She put her arm through Mr. Corstairs's and Lord Hawksmore's arms. She still had to ensure that there were no hard feelings on the part of the other gentlemen. If she was going to make both Lord Felbridge and Julian sorry they had ever toyed with her heart, she needed all the admirers she could get.

They began to slowly walk away from the field through the archery club's garden and toward the guest house. As they walked, Cassandra was sharply reminded of the gardens in Calcutta. It was incredible that the flowers growing here were so similar to the ones in India and yet so different. Somehow their colors were not as vibrant—and certainly, they did not have the same intense smell. It was the one thing that Cassandra truly missed—the smell of the Indian flowers.

"Have you heard about this new man, Huntley, being put up for membership at White's?" Mr. Corstairs asked Lord Hawksmore.

Cassandra looked up. "You met him at my cousin's a few weeks ago, did you not?"

"Ah! That's where I met him!" Mr. Corstairs said, shaking his head. "Knew I'd met him somewhere, but couldn't remember where. Thank you, Miss Renwick." He gave her a warm smile.

Cassandra nodded, and then asked, "So is he going to be allowed to join the club?"

She hoped that she didn't sounded too anxious or concerned. In fact, she sternly told herself, she was not concerned in the least.

"Don't know. We'll have a vote in another week or so. Couple of other fellows have been put up as well."

"I'm certainly not going vote for him. He is an Indian native! He has no business being here and certainly none seeking entrance into a gentlemen's club," Lord Hawksmore said.

"I completely agree," Lord Felbridge said, coming up to them and handing Cassandra her lemonade.

"Do you even know anything about him?" Cassandra asked, resisting the urge to toss her lemonade into Lord Felbridge's face.

He raised his eyebrows at her. "I have spoken to a few friends and they all agree that he is a mushroom, trying to get in where he doesn't belong. Apparently, he did the same thing in Calcutta."

He paused and then narrowed his eyes at Cassandra. "Did you know him there?"

She lifted her chin. "Yes, I did, and he was very well-received by English society," she lied.

"Really? That's not what I heard," he countered.

"Well, your information must be wrong. Even my mother, who is a leader in Calcutta society, invited Lord Huntley to her parties. And now I hear he has inherited quite a fortune along with his father's title, so a mushroom he most certainly is not."

Mr. Corstairs and Lord Hawksmore were impressed. "Well, if that's the case, then there certainly couldn't be anything wrong with his joining White's," Lord Hawksmore said.

"We'll see whether he is accepted as readily here as he was in India," Lord Felbridge retorted, before turning to leave.

Cassandra had never felt so confused. Why had she just defended Julian? What was it to her whether he was accepted here? Yes, she had thought to try to find a way to make him more accepted in Calcutta, and now she had the means to get him accepted here.

But why should she?

Because he does not deserve such treatment, she answered herself. *No one does.*

She continued to saunter down the path with Mr. Corstairs, not paying any attention to what he and Lord Hawksmore were saying to each other.

She remembered how Julian had told her that English society would never accept him because of his skin color. Perhaps he thought that now that he had a title, he would be accepted anyway.

But that shouldn't make any difference to her. Why should she care what he wanted? She refused to admit, even to herself, that it did matter. In fact, it mattered a great deal.

No, she firmly told herself, the real reason she should do her utmost to make Julian socially accepted was that it would help her plan. If he were not invited to any *ton* events, then how was she going to make him fall in love with her, as he had made her do? She would never see him, just as she had not in the past two weeks.

No, she needed him accepted into society. She needed him at hand in order to give him back a taste of his own medicine.

With her mind made up, she noticed Lady Wynworth sitting just outside of the guest house. She had been speaking with Lady Merrick, but now it looked like that lady was being called away.

"If you will excuse me, gentlemen, I believe I will join the ladies," Cassandra said quickly.

Her escorts were perfectly content with this, as they were by now deep into their own conversation.

"Normally, I would not allow you to completely ignore me, as you have been doing," she said with mock severity. "But this time, I will allow it, as I particularly wish to speak with Lady Wynworth."

The gentlemen were about to launch into profuse apologies, but Cassandra held up her hand, gave them a laugh and a wave and turned to grab the seat Lady Merrick had just vacated.

"My lady, you are looking very comfortable here in the shade. Do you mind if I join you?" Cassandra asked as she sat down on the other end of the sofa.

"Why, of course, Miss Renwick. Are you having a pleasant afternoon? Did I see you walking with *both* Mr. Corstairs and the Duke of Hawksmore just now?"

Cassandra gave a little embarrassed laugh. "Yes, they were so kind as to escort me from the archery range. Mr. Corstairs and Lord Merrick were teaching me how to shoot."

"How lovely for you."

"Yes, ma'am," Cassandra said. "Although not nearly as exciting as your ball. I hope I do not sound too eager when I say that I am *so* looking forward to that evening."

Lady Wynworth gave a little condescending smile. "Of course you are, my dear, it is quite natural."

"I imagine that no one would miss it," she said with enthusiasm.

"I am quite pleased with the response I have received so far," the lady conceded.

"Is the new Indian lord going to be in attendance, ma'am? I imagine that whichever party he attends first will become quite the rage!"

Lady Wynworth's eyebrows climbed up a notch on her forehead. "What makes you say that, Miss Renwick?"

"It is just the feeling I get, I suppose. The gentlemen I was with just now were talking of how they were planning on casting their ballots for him to join White's. And I have heard quite a number of other people talking about him as well.

"It is certain that all too soon, everyone will be fighting to have him attend their parties. He is so exotic and unique—why, who ever heard of an Indian-English peer?"

"Indeed." Lady Wynworth looked thoughtful as Cassandra's words sank in, hitting their target right on the bull's-eye.

19

Julian sat alone in his new drawing room, sifting through a pile of notes. Not one of the guests he had invited for dinner had accepted.

He could not understand it. He had invited some of the same gentlemen who had come to his last dinner party, and a few new gentlemen whom he had met while walking in Hyde Park. So why had none of them accepted his invitation?

One simple answer—Fungy and Merry. Last time they had done the inviting. This time Julian had done it on his own.

He had sent round notes of invitation to a dozen men, hoping, even believing, that they would come. But they had all kindly declined their invitations. Previous engagements were the most common excuse, although some did not give any excuse at all but simply stated that they would not be present.

Julian sat back on the sofa. How was he going to get admitted to White's if no one would even attend a simple dinner party he hosted? And if he did not get admitted to White's, it was certain he would never become a member of the *beau monde*.

Without being a member of the *ton*, he would never get to see Cassandra socially, nor would she even consider

marrying him, not when she had some of the most prominent members of society vying for her hand. And then his
life would lose all meaning. He might as well return to Calcutta if he couldn't marry Cassandra—at least there he
had the love of his mother.

Julian shook his head. Well, there was no point in sitting
here feeling sorry for himself. He had to do something.

He suddenly remembered Lady Jersey's soiree, which
Fungy had mentioned as one of the most notable upcoming social events. Most critically, Beau Brummell was
sure to be there. If Julian could secure his approval,
there would be no problem about becoming a member
of White's.

But how was he to get an invitation to one of the season's most sought-after crushes, when his mantle was
bereft of letters of invitation to even the most prosaic
social events?

Julian gave himself another mental shake. He certainly wasn't going to get an invitation by sitting alone in
his drawing room.

He had just stood up when his new manservant came
in bearing a letter. "This just arrived for you, my lord,"
the man intoned.

Julian took the letter. "Thank you, Russell." Breaking
open the seal, he was shocked to find an invitation to
Lady Wynworth's ball two nights hence. She apologized
profusely for the lateness of the invitation, but hoped he
was free that evening.

Julian began to laugh. She hoped that he was free? He
had nothing else on his calendar, nothing at all, so yes,
he supposed he was free.

His luck had turned.

But there was one thing he had to make certain of
before he accepted this invitation. Was Fungy free to
advise him on what he should wear?

If this was to be the beginning of his social career, he
knew that he had to be dressed impeccably to ensure
that it wasn't the end of his career as well. He still didn't

trust his own instincts with regard to fashion. To look right, he needed Fungy.

Cassandra surveyed the ballroom with a languid air. She was getting much better at this, or so Olivia had told her.

She had worn another one of her beautiful sari-dresses—this one made of the pale blue silk sari Gisela had picked out for her. It wasn't nearly as magnificent as the turquoise one, but it was more appropriate for a young, unmarried lady. She noticed another lady with a similarly styled dress, but as it was not actually made out of a sari, it did not have the same appeal. Cassandra supposed she should feel flattered, though, that someone went so far as to copy her.

The beginning strains of a country dance were just starting when Lord Felbridge approached her. After properly acknowledging Lady Bradmore and Olivia, he turned toward her.

"Miss Renwick, that is a most interesting gown," he said, examining her dress rather closely.

"Thank you, sir. Only last week the Prince Regent admired another dress I have in a similar style."

Lord Felbridge looked at her disbelievingly. "Oh come now, you may have had some social successes, but that is doing it too brown, Miss Renwick."

Cassandra raised her chin and snapped open her matching fan. "Believe what you will, my lord."

She then turned away from him and nearly walked into Julian.

Her heart stopped for a moment as she looked up into his dark handsome face and piercing turquoise eyes. She was nearly overwhelmed by his musky sandalwood scent, and then he smiled his brilliant white smile and she knew that she was completely lost.

She quickly called herself to order, however, and noticed that Fungy and Lord Merrick were watching her reaction.

Pulling a smile on to her face, she curtseyed. "Good evening, gentlemen."

They all bowed to her and in unison said, "Good evening, Miss Renwick."

Their perfect timing brought a quick smile to her lips.

It was then that she noticed that something was very different about Julian. She looked at him for a moment, trying to figure out just what it was.

Julian raised his eyebrows and looked at her quizzically and then looked down at himself. "Is there something wrong, Miss Renwick?"

Cassandra could feel her face heat with embarrassment. "Oh, no! No, only . . ."

She then she realized just what it was—he was dressed in the first stare of fashion. In fact, she had never seen him look so fine.

"You look complete to a shade, Julian, er, my lord."

He did. His new, beautifully cut dark clothes set off his coloring magnificently. But more than that, from his carefully tousled hair to his new dancing slippers, he looked like a pink of the *ton*.

What had happened to his claim that fashion did not matter, that he wanted to be accepted just for himself? Hadn't he said as much when they had met in the garden one evening in Calcutta?

Julian bowed elegantly. "I wish you would continue to call me Julian. All this 'my lord'-ing grows tiring after a while, doesn't it? And, I thank you for noticing my new wardrobe."

He then leaned forward and said to her alone, "I had rather hoped that you would."

He gave her the same sweet, secret smile she remembered so well, as if to tell her how much he cared. And in a flash he was the old Julian, her old Julian, again.

She could have sworn that her heart had flipped over in her chest. She gave herself a shake. She should not allow this man to have such an effect on her!

He then blinked and the look in his eyes disappeared, only to be replaced by a twinkle of mischief.

"It is all Fungy's doing, you know," he said a bit more loudly.

Cassandra looked over at Fungy, who was preening a bit. "Well, yes, but shouldn't tell, Huntley," he said, as if sharing a great secret.

"Fungy is much too modest," Lord Merrick said, laughing.

"Yes, indeed. Fungy, you should be proud of your creation," Cassandra said, joining in Lord Merrick's laughter.

"I am! Only Huntley really shouldn't go about telling everyone—not the thing. Must say, I was rather relieved when Huntley came and asked me for help. Clearly couldn't have done it on his own. No offense, old boy, but you've got no fashion sense at all!"

Julian and Merry laughed, but somehow, Cassandra could find nothing to laugh at.

Why did he suddenly *want* to be so fashionable? She hoped it was merely so as to make a good first impression at his first *ton* party.

"I am so sorry, Miss Renwick, I did not forget you, I assure you," Mr. Corstairs said, cutting in.

"Oh, Mr. Corstairs, no, I did not think that you had," Cassandra said, suddenly remembering that she had promised this dance to him.

"Fungy, Merry, how do you do? I do beg your pardon. Shall we?" He put his arm out for Cassandra to take, which she did automatically.

But she had noticed that he had not acknowledged Julian, or, in fact, even looked at him.

Cassandra was led away to dance, wishing that she could say something cutting to Mr. Corstairs for having snubbed Julian in that way. But she could find no way to do so without earning his enmity.

After their dance, she found that she was engaged for the next few dances, as was normally the case. Still, she could not help but look around for Julian whenever she had the chance.

She would invariably find him standing by himself, or with either Fungy or Lord Merrick watching the dancing. She was sharply reminded of her coming-out ball in Calcutta, the first time she had seen him. Then too, he had simply stood alone, watching.

And now, as then, when he would approach someone to be introduced, he was cut more often than he was not.

When she saw Lady Bertram turn her back on him, Cassandra's heart wanted to break. Lady Jersey had looked like she wanted to do the same thing, but since Fungy introduced them, she had no choice but to stand looking very disapprovingly at Julian. Lady Jersey nodded coldly, letting everyone know that Julian was one gentleman who would *not* be receiving vouchers for Almack's.

Cassandra had to forcibly remind herself time and again that she hated Julian. She should *not* be feeling sorry for a man who toyed with her as he had, she sternly reprimanded her heart.

But he looked so lonely and forlorn! She hoped that, like in Calcutta, he would not allow society's reaction to bother him. He had been so brave and strong then in the face of prejudice. Surely he could do the same here, even though she knew he was hurting inside.

It really was a shame, she thought, if he had worn his new clothes in order to be accepted by society. It clearly wasn't working. She hoped that there was another reason for his sudden interest in being fashionable.

Lord Felbridge was just leading her from the floor when there was a flurry of activity as the Prince Regent made a grand entrance.

She and Lord Felbridge watched with equal fascination as Prinny made his way through the crowd, stopping here and there to kiss some lucky lady's hand or have a word with this lord or that. One young girl nearly swooned when His Royal Highness gave her cheek a pat.

He just chuckled and left her to the ministrations of her concerned mama.

"Ah, my dear friend from India!" the prince greeted Cassandra. "Wearing another stunning creation from your sari wardrobe, I see."

He kissed the air above her hand and then looked to see who she was escorted by this evening. "Flatridge, isn't it?" he asked vaguely.

"Felbridge, your Royal Highness, an honor, sir," Lord Felbridge bowed obsequiously.

"Yes, yes. Well, you are a lucky fellow, Felbridge, to be escorting this lovely young thing," he said.

Lord Felbridge bowed once again but stole a sideways glance at Cassandra.

"I beg your pardon, Your Royal Highness, but have you met the Earl of Huntley? He is also from India," Cassandra said quickly.

The prince looked slightly bemused at Cassandra's temerity. "No, is he here tonight?"

"Yes, sir, although I am not certain exactly where."

"Well, one will meet him when one comes across him, no?" he said, and then moved on.

Cassandra watched His Royal Highness greet the next couple a few feet away from them, before turning back to Lord Felbridge.

His mouth was hanging open and he was just gaping at her. Cassandra tried very hard to control her giggles, but some escaped as she thought of the phrase 'you could knock him down with a feather'—for that was exactly what Lord Felbridge looked like.

Very quickly, he pulled himself back together. "My most profound apologies, Miss Renwick. I see now that I was very wrong earlier when I did not believe that Prinny had complimented you on your beautiful gown."

Cassandra tried her hardest not to look smug, but she was afraid that some of what she was feeling seeped through her expression. "It is quite all right, my lord. I'm certain it won't happen again."

She turned and walked back to where her cousin and Aunt Bradmore were standing. A quick glance behind her, however, showed that Lord Felbridge was looking at her with a new light in his eyes.

Clearly he was putting two and two together. Her numerous admirers had caught his attention, else he certainly would not have sought her out himself. And now, with the notice of Prinny, surely he was beginning to see what a mistake he had made in considering her a nobody.

Cassandra felt like putting a little skip in her step— things were working out exactly as she had planned. Felbridge was so predictable.

"The prince stopped to speak to you, Cassandra! What did he say?" Olivia wanted to know immediately as Cassandra reached her side.

"He was kind enough to remember me as his friend from India," she said, and then immediately lowered her voice. "But did you see Lord Felbridge's face afterwards?"

Both she and Olivia began to giggle behind their hands.

"Cassandra, he is speaking to Cousin Huntley!" Olivia whispered urgently, tugging on Cassandra's arm.

She turned around and, indeed, there was the prince looking rather serious as he spoke with Julian. His Royal Highness nodded his dismissal and Julian bowed low as Prinny moved to take Lady Wynworth's hand.

As the music began, the prince led Lady Wynworth out for a country dance. And once again, Julian was left standing by himself, watching people forming sets for the dance.

Without even realizing what she was doing, Cassandra found herself approaching him.

"Julian, would you dance with me?" she heard herself saying.

Julian's eyes widened and then narrowed again with pleasure. He bowed to her. "I would be honored."

He then held out his arm for her and they joined the others making up the dance.

* * *

It was the first time he had danced since coming to London, and how fitting it was that it was with Cassandra—the most wonderful, beautiful young lady at the ball.

Julian had been quite surprised to find how closely the balls in Calcutta matched this one. From the decorations to the people, even to the way he was treated by all of the other guests.

Nothing had changed, he thought grimly. What would it take for people to see him as anything other than a man of mixed blood? Clearly, his new wardrobe was not working as an entrée to society, which he should have known.

It had, however, elicited a response from Cassandra and had thus achieved its purpose.

Cassandra had always been there for him, supporting him when others turned their backs. And here she was again, dancing with him and smiling up at him as if he were the only man in the room.

She truly seemed happy to be with him.

And with her next to him, he was the happiest man alive.

He needed to show her. The urge to tell her right now just how much he loved her nearly overwhelmed him.

He watched her move gracefully through the steps of the dance, giggling at something the gentleman she was with said to her.

No, now was not the time. Now was not the moment he wanted. He should not tell her in public, and he should not just blurt it out to her either.

He wanted the moment he told Cassandra that he loved her and wanted to spend the rest of his life with her to be the most wonderful moment in both of their lives.

When she said yes to him, when she told him out loud—and not just with a look of her eyes or a movement of her hand—just how much she loved him, that would be a moment to savor for the rest of his life. And he would savor it—just as he would savor her and treat her like the very special person that she was—for the rest of their lives.

"Julian, you should take Miss Smithfield's hand and turn her about," Cassandra hissed at him, abruptly pulling him out of his daydream.

He immediately did as he was told, giving the poor Miss Smithfield his most apologetic smile. She did not look entirely convinced, but at least she did not scowl at him.

Julian was shocked by the number of looks he received after that dance. They were looks of appraisal and acceptance from the mamas of many young ladies. They were the very same looks they gave Merry.

Just as an experiment, Julian tried joining in a conversation with Cassandra's friend, Mr. Corstairs, who was standing nearby. He was not turned away.

After a thorough discussion, dominated by Corstairs, on the merits of setting up a stud farm, Julian managed to turn the conversation.

"I say, would you mind terribly, introducing me to . . ." Julian quickly looked around the ballroom and picked a likely young lady, one whom he had seen dancing with many of the young bucks. ". . . to that young lady over there." He nodded in her direction.

Corstairs looked over to where Julian had indicated. "Happy to! Although I must warn you, Miss Price-Liste is known for being in the market for a wealthy husband. Might get caught. I'd be careful if I were you."

Julian smiled. He was certain that the young lady would not care if he were as rich as Prinny.

"I'll take that risk," was all he said to his companion, however.

Julian wasn't sure if he was fortunate or not, but he soon found out that Corstairs had been absolutely correct. He was sized up and appraised by her mama within five minutes of being introduced, and by the end of their dance, invited to call upon her father!

The rest of the evening passed in a haze for Julian. He

suddenly was as sought after as any young wealthy and titled gentleman present.

The one thing he distinctly recalled the next morning, however, was the amount of attention Lord Felbridge began to pay to Cassandra.

Julian didn't like it, not one bit. And he especially didn't like the way Cassandra seemed to revel in it.

20

Cassandra could not believe it—Lord Felbridge calling at ten of the clock! But there it was, his card was in her hand and the footman was waiting for an answer.

She looked to Aunt Bradmore, who sat next to her at the breakfast table. "What do you suppose he wants?"

"At this hour of the morning, Cassandra, there is only one thing that a gentleman wants. Clearly he is here to propose, and after his behavior last night, I am not overly surprised. The question is, what are you going to do?" She took a sip of her tea and waited for an answer.

Cassandra too drank some of her tea, but only as an excuse to postpone answering her aunt's question. She turned to the waiting footman. "Show his lordship into the drawing room and tell him I will be with him momentarily."

She then turned back to Aunt Bradmore. "There is no question that I shall do as I have been planning."

"But is that what you really want, Cassandra? Think about it, my dear. You could be married to a viscount," Aunt Bradmore said, as if trying to tempt a child with a sweet.

Cassandra frowned. "I could not care less if he were a duke. I will not marry Lord Felbridge." With that, she stood up and went to hear what the man had to say for himself.

"My dear Miss Renwick, how good it is of you to see me so early in the morning!" Lord Felbridge greeted her, taking two long strides across the room to grasp hold of her hands.

"Lord Felbridge! I must admit to some curiosity as to what would cause you to call so early," she said, trying to extract her hands from his grip.

"It is nothing short of extreme emotion, I assure you. An emotion so strong I have hardly been able to sleep for it. You must excuse me, but indeed, I have never felt this way before. I hope I am not frightening you by my exuberance?" he asked, looking down at her hands, which she had finally managed to pull out from his.

"Er, no. Not at all. Won't you sit down?" She moved to two straight-backed chairs near the fire and sat in one.

Lord Felbridge sat in the other, but so close to the edge of the chair that he looked like he might fall out of it at any moment.

"Miss Renwick . . . Cassandra, if I may?"

Cassandra gave a slight nod.

"I fear I have wronged you—and only last night did I realize how grievously."

"Oh?"

"Yes. When the prince acknowledged you, I realized what a fool I had been. You see, I have been suppressing my true feelings for you because I thought you not quite my peer. Your father is . . . well, he has a fine position in India, from what I understand, but his birth is not of the highest stature. And so I felt forced by social expectations to turn away from you—to put aside my feelings and to seek out some other young lady of higher birth for my bride."

Cassandra opened her mouth to speak, but he held up his hand and rushed on, "But now . . . now I see that I have no reason to think less of you—and I can, with clear conscience, ask you what I have been longing to for so very long."

He dropped down onto his knee in front of Cassandra. Taking her hand in his, he said, "Cassandra, my love, please, would you look kindly upon this fool and agree to be my wife?"

Fool indeed. She would be a fool to believe all of the nonsense he had just spouted. How dare he claim to have loved her from the very beginning! She knew it was not so. On the other hand, she was not entirely sure that he did not believe himself to be in love with her now.

And that was all that she needed.

She smiled sweetly at the man before her. "Lord Felbridge . . ."

"John," he urged.

"I'm sorry?"

"John. My Christian name is John."

"Oh! Er, John, as much as I appreciate your very kind offer, I am afraid I simply cannot agree to marry a man who would let society dictate his feelings and actions in this way. That society would matter to such an extent that you would put aside the love you feel for me, shows how little you value that love and how little you value me. What matters is not what society thinks about a person, but the person inside and your feelings for them."

Cassandra stood up. Looking down at Lord Felbridge, still on his knee before her, she gave him her final blow. "I deserve better than you, Lord Felbridge. I deserve true love."

Lord Felbridge stood up quickly. He looked stunned. "But . . . I do! . . . you ungrateful . . ." He took a step back as if he couldn't stand to be near her.

"You have just made a huge mistake, Miss Renwick. You have turned down probably the best marriage proposal you will ever receive! Do you really think that Hawksmore will offer for you? He will not! He knows his place and will not allow emotion to rule his head."

Cassandra shook her head, amazed at how deeply she

must have hurt him for him to lash out at her like this. But he mistook her meaning.

"You will see. Hawksmore won't marry you." He gave her an angry smile. "And I would seriously doubt that Merrick could be brought up to scratch either, so you have just passed up your best opportunity to make an advantageous marriage."

"It is not an advantageous marriage I am looking for, Lord Felbridge, but one based on love and mutual respect. Good morning, sir. The footman will see you out." She raised her chin a notch and waited for him to take his leave.

"Then you will be waiting a very long time," he said, before giving her a slight bow and walking out the door.

"Well?" Olivia was waiting in Cassandra's room when she returned there.

"Well, the deed is done. I have turned him down."

"And what was Lord Felbridge's reaction?"

Cassandra shrugged. "It was just as I had expected. He was very upset. He thought himself to be in love with me, made a great speech about it, and then I told him that I would not marry him."

Olivia studied her. One side of her lips curled up into a grim smile. "Somehow you don't seem as happy as one would expect from someone whose carefully planned scheme has just come to fruition."

Cassandra dropped down into a chair and stared into the empty fireplace. "I don't suppose I am. I should be, but somehow I find no great pleasure in hurting him. Even though originally it was he who hurt me."

Resting her elbow on the arm of the chair and her head in her hand, she said quietly, "And now I have to do the same to Julian."

21

Julian looked magnificent and was the epitome of a sophisticated man about town.

It nearly broke Cassandra's heart. She just didn't understand why he had taken to dressing this way.

She had just turned down Felbridge's suit because he cared more for society's opinion than for his own feelings for her. Could it be possible that Julian was the same way? Had the social success he had enjoyed at Lady Wynworth's ball not been enough for him?

She watched as he was approached by matchmaking mamas, all wanting to introduce him to their title-seeking daughters. He bowed and was obviously as charming as he knew how, and the quiet ache in Cassandra's heart grew in intensity.

It wasn't that she wanted him for herself, she forcefully reminded herself. She was not interested in Julian. She was not in love with him. She only wanted revenge.

Yes, perhaps if she kept telling herself this, she would eventually believe it. And perhaps all of the beautiful young ladies with whom Julian was dancing would not fall immediately in love with him as she had.

And perhaps the sky would fall.

Cassandra watched him for as much of the evening as she could. It was difficult, as she was also rather sought

after—dancing and being paid court to by any number
of gentlemen. But despite her own popularity, she could
not find any enjoyment in the evening or keep her eyes
from straying toward Julian.

Her one consolation was that he seemed to be having
the same problem. As their eyes met yet again across the
dance floor, Julian finally made a move.

His journey around the room was frustratingly slow, as
he stopped to speak to various people along the way. Finally, however, he reached her side.

"Miss Renwick, I could not help but notice that you
are looking a little flushed. Would you care to take a
breath of fresh air?" he said, stepping in between Lord
Hawksmore and Mr. Corstairs.

"How very thoughtful of you, my lord. I would appreciate that." She put her hand into his outstretched one
and allowed him to lead her away.

"I say, Miss Renwick, had you not promised the next
dance to me?" Mr. Corstairs objected.

"I am sorry, sir, you will have to forgive me," she said,
pausing briefly to give him an apologetic smile. Her desire
to be with Julian overwhelmed her, even to the point of
being rude to poor Mr. Corstairs. He would forgive her,
she was sure of it.

The garden was cool and dark as Cassandra allowed
Julian to slowly walk her down a pathway, away from the
hot and noisy house.

They stopped just under the broad branches of a large
oak tree. The setting reminded her forcefully of the last
time they had stood together under a tree—near the
Hindu temple, on that beautiful day when he had showed
her just how much he had cared.

"You are looking beautiful this evening, Cassandra,"
Julian said, taking her hands in his own.

Somewhere along the way he had taken off his gloves.
Cassandra wished she could have done the same in
order to feel the rough maleness of his hands as she had
when he had touched her under the banyan tree. As it

was, she could feel the heat of his hands even through her own gloves.

"And you are dressed as impeccably as you have been since you entered London society."

He nodded, smiling down at her, clearly taking her words for a compliment, although she was not sure that she meant them as one. She was still worrying about the implication of his clothes, although it was becoming difficult to remember much of anything with his strong male presence so close to her.

But then he took another step nearer, and she could smell his delicious sandalwood scent.

It pushed all of her fears and thoughts to the back of her mind.

"Your sari-inspired dresses seem to have become quite the rage," he said, his deep voice sending small shivers through her.

"It is funny how people have copied them, isn't it?"

"It is because you look so elegant in them, just as you did in the sari you wore to the bazaar in Calcutta."

Cassandra smiled, knowing that she must be flushing at his praise. But she was truly thrilled that he still remembered that day and all of their time together in Calcutta. She still did. They were the best days of her life—a time when she could truly be herself.

"It is so much nicer to be here in England, though," he continued. "And to be here with you."

"Julian . . ."

"I love you, Cassandra," he said with such fervent honesty that Cassandra wanted to cry with joy.

"The only thing that could make me any happier right now," he continued, "is if you would agree to be my wife."

"Julian, you don't know how long I have waited to hear you say that! You don't know how difficult it has been for me to see you as you are now and know how much I loved you."

Then, to her dismay, she felt tears slipping down her cheeks. "This is so hard for me," she whispered.

"It shouldn't be hard at all . . ."

"No, Julian, it is. I loved you so much when we were in Calcutta."

"As I love you. And now we can marry—there are no more barriers between us. Everything will be just as it should be."

Cassandra covered her face with her hands. She loved him so much, and yet she *had* to spurn him.

How could she do this to him?

"Cassandra, now that I have become accepted into society, it will be perfect. I now have a title, money, social standing . . ." he said, taking her hands again.

Cassandra caught her breath. What was he saying?

"We can have a big society wedding," he continued hurriedly. "We can invite everyone, even Prinny . . ."

Cassandra jumped back. She felt a sharp pain slice through her head.

Through the fog of her surprise and pain, she lashed out at him. "Is that all that matters to you now? Is that all that you care about? Prinny? And what society thinks?" She pulled her hands out of his.

"Isn't that what you want?"

"No! I don't care about the *ton*."

"But the way you behave . . . the way you dress . . . your beaus . . ." Julian was clearly as confused by her behavior as she was by his.

"I did that to get revenge on Lord Felbridge for calling me a nobody. Why have *you* fawned over society?"

"For you. Because . . . because I thought that that was what you wanted."

"What I want is the man I fell in love with in Calcutta. I want the real Julian Ritchie, not this coxcomb that you have become."

"But this is not the real me. You know that."

"Do I? How do I know that? You've lied to me before, Julian. You used me when we were in Calcutta. . . ."

"Cassandra, I am telling you the truth! I love you. I only did this for you."

"How do I know that, Julian? How do I know that this time you are being honest with me?"

Julian took a step back from her. He had nothing to say.

A sob broke from Cassandra, and she turned and ran away before she embarrassed herself entirely, leaving Julian behind in the deepening gloom of the trees.

22

Fungy and Merry found Julian more than halfway through a bottle of brandy when they came looking for him at his rooms later that evening.

"Wondered what happened to you this evening. Wanted to have a word on how you deal with Brummell at Lady Jersey's party. Be the making of you," Fungy said, helping himself to what was left of Julian's brandy.

"Sorry for leaving without a word," Julian said, barely looking up from his drink.

Merry and Fungy exchanged a curious look.

"All right, out with it," Merry said, his casual lounging against the mantelpiece belying the concern in his voice.

Julian looked over at him and then finished the rest of the brandy in his glass. With a grim smile on his face he said, "I proposed to Miss Renwick this evening."

"Turn you down?" Fungy said, clearly surprised at this news.

Julian briefly related all that had happened between him and Cassandra since they had first met in Calcutta and then all that she had said to him that evening.

Fungy was left with his mouth hanging open. "Just because you want to be accepted by the *ton* and wear fashionable clothes doesn't mean you're not being honest," he said, indignantly.

Merry gave a little laugh. "Indeed, Fungy is right, although I can see how she could still be angry with you for having used her."

"I know," Julian said. "The worst of this is that I do not blame her for having turned me down. I did use her. I used her to gain acceptance into society."

"But that was in Calcutta. You didn't do that here," Merry protested.

"No, but I have not been completely honest here either. I have allowed others to dictate what I do," he nodded towards Fungy, "and what I wear."

Fungy sat up straighter, looking at him with wide eyes.

"I know, I know. I asked you to tell me what to wear. I asked you to make me fashionable. But that is not truly what is important to me."

He got up to refill his glass from the near-empty bottle. Then he stood staring at his drink, thinking over this problem. "What I've got to do now is to prove to Cassandra that I have changed. That I no longer care for society," he said, thinking aloud.

"And how are you going to do that? It will take time, Julian." Merry poured out the last glass from the brandy.

"I don't believe that it will. I've got an idea." Julian got up and pulled out another bottle of brandy from the stash inside of his cabinet. Opening it, he refilled all of their glasses. He then raised his glass to salute his friends, knowing full well that what he was going to do might not be the most prudent course of action.

But it was what he had to do.

"Cassandra, it is enough!" Aunt Bradmore pulled back the covers of Cassandra's bed from where they had been covering her head.

"No, it is not. It will never be," Cassandra moaned.

"Really, my girl, two days is certainly long enough to recover from a plot of your own making."

"Yes, Cassandra, you are the one who decided to take

your revenge on Cousin Huntley. You can't now be so very upset when you were successful in your own plan." Olivia, sitting on the counterpane next to Cassandra, smoothed Cassandra's hair away from her face.

"I know, but I honestly hadn't expected that I would still be in love with him. Or that it would hurt so much!"

Aunt Bradmore sighed. "Well, my dear, there is only one solution to a tumble. You must get right back up again."

"But Aunt Bradmore . . ."

"No, Cassandra, I am tired of your complaints about how your heart is broken. I have given you plenty of time to get over this. Now it is time for you to get up and re-enter society. You cannot miss Lady Jersey's soiree. If you do so, you will never see another voucher to Almack's, and you will harm your cousin's chances of obtaining one as well."

Cassandra groaned. She could not do that to Olivia, and Aunt Bradmore knew that she never would. She ducked her head back down under her covers once again, knowing the battle was lost.

It was a very sad-looking young lady who entered Lady Jersey's soiree that evening. The face powder Lady Brad-more had lent to her did somewhat cover up the red still rimming her blue eyes, but there was little anyone could do about the smile that just would not come to her face. Try as hard as she might, Cassandra just could not muster one up.

Olivia did her best to draw attention away from her usually vibrant cousin, but she just did not have the same energy that Cassandra had naturally.

"I am so happy to hear that you are feeling better, Miss Renwick," Lord Hawksmore said, gently taking her hand and kissing the back of it.

"Still looking a trifle peaked, but so glad you could make it," Mr. Corstairs said, lingering near her as well.

She gave them her best approximation of a smile.

"You are both so good to me. I do not deserve such fine friends."

"Not at all."

"Can I get you some lemonade?" Mr. Corstairs offered.

"Thank you, that would be lovely," Cassandra replied softly, sitting down in the chair brought forward for her by Lord Hawksmore.

She was glad that Aunt Bradmore had put it about that she had been indisposed. Still, it was very reassuring to have her two most devoted suitors still by her side.

Lord Hawksmore was doing an excellent job regaling her with all of the gossip of the last two days while she sipped her lemonade. He even managed to move Julian to the back of her mind for moments at a time, although she could never completely forget about him.

She was smiling at an amusing anecdote the duke was relating when she noticed Lord Merrick and Fungy hurrying in. They stopped just inside the door, their eyes roaming the room. As soon as they caught sight of her, they both sped over.

"Miss Renwick, I am so glad to see you! Thank God, you are here," Lord Merrick and Fungy said in unison while approaching her.

"Good evening, gentlemen, is something amiss?" Cassandra asked, sitting up. She did not like the looks of grave concern on both of their faces.

"Something amiss? I should say something is amiss!" Fungy said emphatically.

"Hawksmore, Corstairs, you must excuse Miss Renwick. We need her services most desperately," Lord Merrick said, taking Cassandra's hand and helping her stand up.

"But what is the matter?" Lord Hawksmore asked with alarm.

"Huntley's attempting social suicide." Fungy placed his hand on the small of Cassandra's back, urging, almost pushing, her forward.

"We can only hope that Miss Renwick will be able to convince him to stop." Lord Merrick tucked her hand into the crook of his arm and led her away, leaving the stunned gentlemen behind them.

As they walked quickly from the main drawing room, Cassandra looked from one man to the other. "Is Julian all right? What has he done? What do you mean by social suicide?"

But *you'll see* was the only answer she could get from the two very determined men.

Instead of turning toward the front door, they pulled her around toward the back of the stairs, where there was a large display of ferns and potted palms.

Just as they approached, Julian stepped out from behind the plants. "I am not waiting any longer . . ." he began to say and then stopped short at the sight of Cassandra.

He was dressed in his old buff-colored pantaloons, yellow coat and his blue-and-yellow-striped waistcoat. His boots were old and scuffed and did not look as if they had seen polish for some time. In short, he looked precisely as he had when Cassandra had met him in Calcutta.

Choking back a combined sob and laugh, Cassandra covered her mouth and fiercely tried to blink away the tears that were immediately threatening to fall from her eyes.

"You see what we mean!" Fungy said, mistaking her reaction for one of horror.

"You've got to convince him that he can't be seen in public like this," Lord Merrick said, pleading with her with his eyes.

"Not tonight! Got to make a good impression tonight. Brummell will be here!" Fungy was looking close to tears himself.

All Cassandra could do was to shake her head, her hand still covering her mouth.

She had known at once what Julian had done. She knew the meaning of these clothes, and it was, as his friends had said, social suicide.

He had done this for her.

In front of her, with his friends looking on, Julian dropped down on one knee. "Cassandra, I don't care about Beau Brummell. I don't care if I never become a member of White's. You are all I care about. You are all I have ever cared about since I've come to know you."

"Don't forget about the apology for using her," Lord Merrick whispered loudly to Julian.

"Or the fact that it is important to be well-dressed," Fungy put in.

Cassandra's eyes shifted between the two men as she stifled her laughter. Sheer joy welled up inside her.

Julian stood up, looking like he was going to do some serious harm to his friends. "Could you two please give us a moment of privacy? I can handle this!"

"Didn't last time," Fungy said, but then he was quickly hushed by Lord Merrick and forcibly pulled away.

Julian took her hand and pulled Cassandra back behind the potted plants for more privacy.

It was darker there and smelled earthy and fresh. Cassandra, looking up into Julian's eyes, feeling his warmth so close to her, could easily forget she was standing in Lady Jersey's entryway.

"Cassandra . . ."

"You want to apologize?" she asked, giggling.

Julian laughed, his shoulders coming down a touch with the relief of his tension. "Yes, for being such a cad in using you."

Cassandra nodded. "And Fungy will be horribly upset if you are not dressed to perfection."

"Yes, poor Fungy. He was so proud of his creation."

"As well he should have been. You looked wonderful, Julian."

"But you prefer the true me."

"Yes. Of course, if the true you also includes being dressed more fashionably than this, I must say I would not mind so very much. Just so long as you are honest with me."

"Always and forever, I swear. Just say that you love me and will marry me."

"Julian, I love you. And I *will* marry you."

She looked up at him and let herself be pulled into that deep turquoise place that was Julian's eyes. His love for her shone so clearly through them.

He put his hand to her cheek, letting his rough thumb gently caress her soft skin. "And I love you, Cassandra, and I want to spend the rest of my life with you."

His words flowed over her like a ray of sunshine, making her feel warm and cherished.

He bent closer to her. His lips brushed against hers very softly at first, but then they settled down and he took full possession of her mouth. And she gave it to him, willingly, with all of the love she felt for him.

Her mind went blank and simply exalted in all of the wonderful feelings that were running through her heart and body. She felt such new and delicious sensations as his hands softly caressed her back, her sides, her breasts. A shiver of excitement went through her.

She pressed herself against him and felt his hard male body against hers. She could not get close enough, but wriggled and pressed against him in an effort to get nearer.

A moan escaped from his throat and he pulled back, leaving Cassandra feeling suddenly cold away from his heat.

Cradling her face with his hands, Julian smiled down at her. "That will have to wait until after we are married, my love."

"Then let's get married soon."

"Yes. As soon as possible," he said, lowering his lips to hers once again.

This time she pulled away. "But let's not invite Prinny."

They laughed, immersed in their shared love and understanding, until Cassandra impatiently pulled Julian's lips to hers once more.

Dear Reader,

I hope you have enjoyed this slightly different take on the traditional Regency.

Life in Calcutta (recently renamed Kolkata), a city entirely created by the British, has been a fascination for me ever since I married a son of that city. It is a city rich in history, having been the capital of British India for many years.

Even today, you can see the legacy of British life in the styles of houses, names of major streets throughout the city, and the little enclaves of colonial life which still exist—the country clubs and the Royal Calcutta Turf Club (where horse races are held every week in season). It is a fascinating city, growing and modernizing and yet staying true to its identity as a city of India.

This book is one of a quartet, each featuring one of four close friends. Merry's story can be found in my first book, *Miss Seton's Sonata*, and is also touched upon in my second book, *Wooing Miss Whately*. *Wooing Miss Whately* features "Sin" (Sinclair Stratton, Viscount Reath), who at the time of Julian's book was in Delhi on a diplomatic mission and so was not mentioned (but I'm sure he was in Merry's and Fungy's hearts and minds). And finally, in September 2005, Fungy's book, *Dame Fortune*, will be coming out. It promises to be as fun as he is.

By the way, the correct chronological order of the books is actually Julian's book, then *Wooing Miss Whately*, followed by *Miss Seton's Sonata* and finally, Fungy's book.

Please look for all of these books wherever you normally buy books. More information on them, the Regency period, and Kolkata can be found at www.meredithbond.com. Please write to me at P.O. Box 341413, Bethesda, MD 20827.

Meredith

More Regency Romance
From Zebra